The Hot Spots

Also edited by J. H. Blair

THE GOOD PARTS

The Hot Spots

THE BEST EROTIC WRITING IN MODERN FICTION

edited by
J. H. BLAIR

BERKLEY BOOKS, NEW YORK

A Berkley Book
Published by The Berkley Publishing Group
A division of Penguin Putnam Inc.
375 Hudson Street
New York, New York 10014

Book design by Tiffany Kukec
Cover design by Erika Fusari
Cover photograph by Alvin Booth

PRINTING HISTORY
Berkley trade paperback edition / July 2001

The Penguin Putnam Inc. World Wide Web site address is
www.penguinputnam.com

Library of Congress Cataloging-in-Publication Data
The hot spots / [compiled by] J.H. Blair.
p. cm.
Includes bibliographical references.
ISBN 0-425-17837-4
1. Erotic stories, American. I. Blair, J.H. II. Title.

PS648.E7 H68 2001
813'.50803538—dc21
00-065196

PRINTED IN THE UNITED STATES OF AMERICA

10 9 8 7 6 5 4 3 2 1

CONTENTS

Contents

Contents

INTRODUCTION

Hot Spots of the Twentieth Century

THE LAST DECADE OF THE TWENTIETH CENTURY—WHAT MANY HAVE called the American Century—was a time when most Americans were simultaneously looking backward and looking forward: Where have we been? Where are we going? Writers of serious fiction were (no surprise) at the forefront of this collective national stock-taking and much of the best erotic writing reflects this.

With the collapse of the Soviet Union, for the first time in the century there was only one superpower in the world. Looking back on the 1900s, one historically-minded cartoonist drew three gravestones: *European order—died 1918; fascism—died 1945; communism—died 1989.* Only capitalism has survived. When commentators and scholars were listing the reasons for this, did anyone mention erotica? Stalin, Hitler, and Mussolini tried to remake the world by remaking the human body. Flesh was constantly contorted and perpetually refunctioned until it became a signifying machine. But in America, flesh stayed flesh. To cut it another way: there are no memorable love scenes in communist or fascist fiction.

Let me go back a bit to one small but typical example. In 1928, a group of young French journalists, scholars, and intellectuals traveled to Rome, Moscow, and New York. When they wrote about their experiences in these three cities, Moscow and Rome were seen as boldly visionary capitals—both capable of challenging time itself by creating new utopian civilizations. The writers wondered: Would the future be communist or fascist? Liberal, bourgeois democracy was seen as hopelessly antiquated and outmoded, incapable of providing the inventive newness that the twentieth century demanded. New York was harshly criticized as the soulless center of a vulgar modernity that was "eradicating authenticity." One writer singled out three things in particular that he found most objectionable about Manhattan. There were too many cars. There were too many new buildings that, unlike the new architectural spirit of Rome or Moscow, which exalted the state, were merely monuments to money. And, there were too many women who cared only about shopping for clothes and listening to the latest jazz and Tin Pan Alley tunes.

Compare this with the section of E. L Doctorow's *Billy Bathgate*, which came out in 1989, the very year communism collapsed, in which Billy, the fifteen-year-old from Dutch Schultz's inner circle, is riding through the streets of New York. He cracks open a window and smells the fresh rainy night air. He is intoxicated by the cacophony of the city—the bells of the streetcars remind him of the mayhem of a prizefight; the very equestrian statues in Central Park seem to be slogging through the rain-swept streets. Soon, the Packard stops at the Savoy-Plaza Hotel, and Billy gets out to accompany Dutch Schultz's mistress, Drew Preston. They run into the hotel, and though they spent only a moment or two in the teeming rain, they're drenched. Once inside, they find themselves in a splendid lobby. Billy goes on to describe the Savoy-Plaza: It was the kind of hotel where when the elevator door opened they were already in the apartment. Billy looks around the suite and is awestruck by the luxury:

> *I was left standing at the doorway looking into a room that was a private library with a glass-enclosed bookcase and a tall leaning ladder that rolled on rails and an immense globe in its own polished wood framework, and light that came from two brass table lamps with green shades at either end of a soft sofa . . .*

He is taken with everything in the suite, but especially by the white telephone on the table:

> *I had never seen a white phone before. Even the cord was wound in white fabric. The big bed had a white upholstered headboard and big fluffy pillows, about half a dozen of them, with little lace skirts, and all the furniture was grey and the thick carpet was grey and the lights were hidden and shown out of a cornice onto the walls and ceiling. Two people used this room because there were books and magazines on both end tables, and two immense cabinets with white doors and curving white legs that were closets inside, his and hers, and two matching dressers with his shirts and her underwear, and until now I only knew about wealth what I had read in the tabloids, and I thought I could imagine, but the detailed wealth in this room was amazing, to think what people really needed when*

they were wealthy, like long sticks with shoehorns at the end on them, and sweaters of every color of the rainbow, and dozens of shoes of every style and purpose, and sets of combs and brushes, and carved boxes with handfuls of rings and bracelets, and gold table clocks with pendulum balls that spun one way, paused, and then spun the other way.

But then he turns his attention to Miss Preston and describes her with the same practical fascination as he had for the furniture:

And then the lady came out of the bathroom with a big towel around her and tucked in under the clavicle, and another towel wrapped around her head like a turban.

Billy watches her dress:

She stood at the armoire and let the big towel fall, and she was altogether taller and longer-waisted and maybe her ass was a little softer and flatter, but there was the prominent spinal column of tender girl bones of my dirty little Rebecca, and all the parts were as Rebecca's parts and the sum was the familiar body of a woman, I don't know what I'd been expecting but she was a mortal being with flesh pinked by the hot bath water, she hooked on her great garter belt and stood on each thin white leg while she gently but efficiently raised the other to receive its sheer stocking, which she pulled and smoothed upward taking care to keep the seam straight till she could lower her toe-wiggling foot and sling her hip and attach the stocking to the metal clips hanging from the garter belt, and then she raised one foot and stepped into her white satin step-ins and then the other, and yanked them up and snapped the waistband, and it was the practiced efficiency of the race of woman dressing, from the assumption they had always made that a G-string was their armor in the world, and that it would do against wars, riots, famines, floods, droughts, and the flames of the arctic night. As I watched, more and more of her was covered, a skirt was dropped over the hips and zipped along the side, two high-heeled shoes were wiggled into, and then dressed only from the waist down and with the towel still on her head, she commenced to pack, going from drawers to armoire to valise and back.

Notice that Doctorow's chapter contains the same three elements singled out for chastisement by the French journalist/intellectual in the 1928 *Revue Française*. There is a car ride. There is a modern building that has nothing to do with glorifying the state and instead is given over to private pleasures. And there is the thoroughly modern clothes-loving city woman. The inevitable triumph of capitalism is contained in Doctorow's details, in the conflation of place, setting, material furnishing, and sensual corporeality. Socialism versus the bracing smell of a rainy New York night from inside a sleek Packard. Communism versus the welcoming warmth of the Savoy-Plaza lobby. Fascism versus a turbaned Drew Preston pulling and smoothing her stockings to keep the seams straight. No contest. The grandiose utopian fantasies of totalitarian regimes never stood a chance against the sexiness of a fast car, a hotel room, a beautiful woman.

All this is very much a part of the American ethos, that uniquely capitalist desire to immerse oneself completely and without remorse in the sensuality of the moment. That ethos—scorned at the beginning of the century but triumphant in the end—invigorates our culture no less than our fiction. We are a society in love with our passions, whether they are cars, luxury hotel rooms, or the voyeuristic desire to hear the sins and errors of other people's lives. And as we venture further into material extravagance and "tell-all" television, we are coming closer and closer to eroticizing the everyday. In return, our erotica is coming closer and closer to reflecting our actual lives.

Something else that neither fascism nor communism could compete with is America's romance of the road. To get in your car and just go, that is the opportunity America offers. Invariably this feeling of freedom includes sexuality. To add an adjective to Shakespeare's famous line, most Americans feel that "highway journeys end in lovers meeting." This became a pervasive motif in the fiction of the 1990s. Dominic Stansberry, who calls to mind the "classic California" passages of Raymond Chandler, uses the highway in his novel *The Last Days of Il Duce*, which, despite its title, does not take place in the 1940s. As the couple tools down Route 101, passing the small towns of Milbrae, San Bruno, Daly City, Sunnyvale, and Mountain View, past the ragged little stuccos that sit hunched along the freeway; past the bowling alleys and motels on one side, the flats on the other, where dozens of men shoveled concrete fill for new industrial parks, they become aware of the vast expanse of the American landscape, how one can drive for hours through a barely varied landscape and never worry about crossing a border or trespassing on someone else's history. It's not like that anywhere else in the world, and American writers were the first to notice it. Writers of the nineties saw even more clearly how sexy this expansiveness was, as if unbounded driving was fueling the libido—one fuel gauge going up while the other winds down.

After a while, the couple comes to an old orchard that is becoming a development. The just-built houses and the fresh black pavement evoke desire.

> *At the end of the path were the houses. They looked to be new houses, built in the last year or so, and the streets were fresh and black. In the orchard you could see the surveyor's lines; the small sticks and the red flags and white string marking out how the street would continue on and join the highway back where we had parked. I caught up to Marie and we looked at the houses, how the street just stopped in the middle of that orchard. Some kids played on the street in front of the houses, a hawk circled overhead, and I wanted Marie more than ever: to take her inside one of those houses and lay with her on the floor and listen to the cry of that hawk and the sound of those children playing.*

Only in America.

And not just in California, either. In Rick Moody's *Purple America*, a motorcycle ride through New London, Connecticut, becomes both an end-of-century recapitulation of New England's once-glorious Industrial Revolution and a contemporary American prelude to a kiss:

Acceleration being the drug of choice under the circumstances, Jane Ingersoll races out of town, shaking the scorched leaves from the autumnal trees past the old, ramshackle Victorians where the seafarers of New London once put into port, those old rooming houses on the hill, lately inhabited by the hard-luck underclasses of Connecticut's crumbling cities, gang kids and their terrorized parents, the unemployed, the elderly, until they're out by the chain stores, the auto dealerships, thirty or forty miles an hour above posted limits, *until Dexter and Jane Ingersoll are rocketing along the swerve of the shore, passing station wagons on the left, panel trucks on the right, failing to signal in the centrifugal thrust of their turns, the squeal of their tires, beside the great rail beds of the northeastern corridor and along old mariners' bars, following the course of the Thames River, back from the mouth of the harbor, watching the mesmeric lights of the port reflect upon the river, until Jane Ingersoll doglegs to the right at the railroad station, past the army recruitment center, bounces over the tracks, grazes a shingle on an empty guardhouse at the edge of a parking lot—and guns it onto the public pier of New London. Out onto the pier! With the bridge span above them, where the after-hours scofflaws aim for Boston before closing time. Raitliffe finally tumbles off the back of the Honda, skinning a palm. Across the rippling currents, now, is the backdrop to this contemporary romance, monument to all that's great in Americans,* Electric Boat, a Division of the General Dynamics Corporation, *where in the dry docks, in show business spotlights, for all to see, are constructed* Polaris *submarines. Cranes poised about them like industrial handmaidens, tawny abominations, the pride of southeastern*

Connecticut, where New England's remaining working men and women—excepting the ones behind the counters of the adult bookshops and the package stores—clock in to build weapons of destruction.

Moody's rhythm is flawless. The first extremely long sentence as he catalogs the details of crumbling Connecticut and contrasts it with New London's once-glorious Victorian seafaring past. Then the exhilarated burst of "Out onto the pier!" followed by the surreal nightscape of "mesmeric lights . . . upon the river" and the huge, looming cranes. After Hex Raitliffe falls off the motorcycle, Jane tells him:

"In the winter, the kids fishtail their cars out here, at the end of the pier, to see who can get closest to driving into the river."

And Hex (who has a bad stutter) says:

"I—w-w-want to k-k-k-k-k-k- . . . I w-w-want to k-k-k-k-k-k-kiss you," and Jane laughs. She shuts off the bike, kicks the kickstand. On the pier against the stage set of ferryboats and dredging barges and coast guard vessels, with wharf rats slipping in and out of view, Jane pulls off her helmet. I feel like a kid again, *Raitliffe says. She draws nigh. In the sandblasted and sea-worn red brick of New London with the nuclear-equipped fishing vessels of the millennium, in the city of fissioning Yankees, Hex Raitliffe, cramping from the cold, fighting off post-nasal drip—kisses his beloved.*

It's all so grubby, isn't it, and yet so sensuous—but then, Moody is telling us, one leads to the other.

OF COURSE, JUST AS THE OPEN ROAD LEADS TO THAT BRIGHT, SHINING newness so beloved by Americans, it also leads back into the past. In this passage from Sue Miller, her protagonist heads homeward at dusk accompanied by the ghost of a long-gone love.

> *Lottie had seen a studio photograph of him at that age, holding his clarinet. He paid for the picture himself. He had thought that he might become a musician. In it, he's wearing a dark suit, his hair is pomaded wetly back. He is unbelievably long and skinny, but there's a sense, too, of something knowing, something hungry about him that stirred Lottie when she held the photograph, even all those long years afterwards. The excitement of those days had folded into Jack's love of music, even into his love of dancing. Once when they were moving together to a swing-band tune at the hotel ballroom in Chicago, he bent over Lottie and whispered, "Care to dance?" and when she'd said yes, they'd walked straight off the slick floor to the front desk and rented a room.*

Lottie has taken a painkiller for a toothache and she starts to feel its effect just as night is coming on.

> *She's in New Jersey now on Route 80, floating on the Percocet. She can still feel the pain. A light, steady throb from under the tooth, actually, but it almost seems to be happening to another*

Lottie, another Charlotte. Dusk has deepened into near-dark along the highway, but there's still a light past the sky. The dark moving shapes of the trees are silhouetted against it. She asked for the directions when she crossed the George Washington Bridge, and she has made every connection, feeling a peace and accomplishment simply in driving, in making this curve, in signaling so politely to change lanes. Traffic was heavy around New York, but it has cleared out now, and she takes comfort in the distant taillights ahead of her, the headlights that move up from behind and sweep the past.

By now it may seem that we've developed a nasty little fetish, a prurient interest, in traffic and the open road. But that's nothing new. It's what the unique brand of American provincialism spawned: When you're given a landscape without end, the bearings in your head expand and connect you in the deepest way to your surroundings. That's what gives these erotic musings context. The mind wanders over the psychic landscape as the asphalt snakes across the featureless countryside.

Shortly thereafter, Lottie turns the radio on, and as she switches stations, Sue Miller takes the reader back and forth across thirty-plus years of American history.

She finds another oldies station but tires of it quickly. They seemed to specialize in white boys—Ricky Nelson, Frankie Avalon. She pushes the seek button, settles on the first clear station, a call-in show. They're discussing the effects of crack cocaine on kids in the ghetto. There's an expert, of course, full of statistics. His voice is nasal, nerdy. Lottie would put money on it, he's never done drugs. Crack is cheap, he says. It's highly addictive, it's the beginning of the end . . . The calls start now on the radio. Gradually the tone of the show changes. Nobody is forcing these kids to use it. Nobody's excluding them from the American dream, if they just get off their asses and go to work. The talk show host is on the callers' side. Maybe addicts deserve their fate. Lottie changes the station. She finds some soft rock, then an Elvis retrospective; the Las Vegas years. She turns the radio off. The Percocet isn't making her sleepy at all. Just somehow tranquil in absolute control.

Ricky Nelson and Frankie Avalon, of course, evoke memories of innocent teen American circa 1959. *American Bandstand*. Dick Clark. Rock 'n' roll with all its Dionysian elements removed to produce safe, sanitized schlock for perky maltshop pinheads. The talk show on crack yanks us back to the present day. Although music is never mentioned, the mere use of the word "crack" calls to mind the violent lyrics of gangsta rap. Then: soft rock—the present-day version of Ricky Nelson and Frankie Avalon—prefabricated vapidity, mall music. Finally Elvis. The early and mid-1970s. The very moment when Las Vegas was starting its journey from a "rat pack" and Chicago mob town to the world's largest family entertainment/theme-park center. Sue Miller has skillfully reproduced the last fifty years of the American experience. And it all started with that erotic memory.

How much of this is real and how much is (possibly pathological) fancy? Are these connections the devilish work of idle minds? I don't think so. Consider one more interesting example:

Laura Kasischke's *Suspicious River*, in which her protagonist is driving to an abortion clinic:

> *It was a three-hour drive to Grand Rapids, a two-laned highway through a tunnel of pines. A deer ran across the road outside Ottawa City, white tail flagging and falling in front of our car, then vanished into the woods on the other side of the highway, and I slowed down after that, afraid I'd come that close to hitting another. I'd been so near to that one I could see the sleek muscles tensing on either side of its ribs as it ran. My father was asleep with his mouth open in the passenger's seat beside me. The weather was cool for May, but bright as milk and shimmering with new leaves. Further, then, outside Ottawa City, I saw two black puppies sprawled in dirt at the side of the road beneath some dusty wildflowers wagging baby blue above their corpses. The puppies looked peaceful there, like boots, not bloody and ruined like roadkill. They looked as if someone had flung them, dead already, out the window of a slow-moving car. Here and there a turkey vulture soared and spiraled. A crow landed on a telephone wire, buoying it with black weight, while the milkweed pods just nodded at each other in the ditches, dumb as swans.*

As she continues to drive, she starts to notice the shacks of the Mexican migrants who have come north to work the fields.

> *The cauliflower field between Suspicious River and the Grand Rapids were dank that day, and every few miles there were clusters of small migrant shacks huddled at the edges of those*

fields. No windows, and their plywood sides had gone grey-green, maybe rotten, through the winter and spring rain. Soon they would be back—dark-haired children licking Popsicles and thin men with straw hats scattered around the shacks. Occasionally a migrant family might be seen at the grocery store in Suspicious River, looking shy and tired under the bright lights in the narrow aisles crowded with cans, holding the little ones' hands. But they were seen rarely, and never anywhere but the grocery store—except out there in those fields, like a human crop.

It takes only a dozen-plus sentences for Kasischke to nail her part of America. Her selection of animal and nature details is perfect. The protagonist is so close to the deer, running scared across the highway, that she "could see the sleek muscles tensing on either side of its ribs." There are two dead puppies, a vulture, and a crow, "dusty wildflowers wagging baby blue" and "milkweed pods dumb as swans." Clearly nature offers no solace. It merely reinforces the bleak hopelessness of roadside rust-belt America. Similarly, human relationships. The headstrong industrial past is her father. "Asleep with his mouth open in the passenger's seat" and the future is "dark-haired children licking Popsicles." A perfect mood for a self-destructive and depressed woman driving to an abortion clinic.

ALTHOUGH MOST AMERICAN WRITERS OF SERIOUS FICTION IN THE 1990s concentrated on the here and now—the U.S.A. at the century's end—some found inspiration in other places and other times. In *One of Us*, Davie Freeman conjures up the heady, intoxicatingly sensual world of pre-war Cairo:

> *The harem wasn't quite what it sounded like to us. The Queen, who was about forty, lived in great luxury there attended by her ladies-in-waiting, who were social figures in their own right and who lived outside the Palace, though they also retained apartments in the harem. They came and went, bringing rumor and gossip. The first, Madame Zulficar, was one of Naali's class and the mother of a young daughter often mentioned as a possible wife for Farouk. The other was Miriam Rolo, who was married to a businessman who was a financial adviser to the King. The Rolos were Sephardic Jews, pillars of the haute Juiverie. Miriam had been in Alexandria with the Queen at Ras-el-tin while I was in Montazeh, though I didn't meet her until Abdin. She was a tall, elegant woman with olive skin that appeared Egyptian but was, in fact, Spanish coloring. She had a high forehead and eyebrows that were more drawn than grown. It gave her a theatrical quality that held great interest for me.*

Of course Farouk's harem is the perfect setting for Miriam's "theatrical quality."

> *Miriam was related to most of the old Sephardic families. She was of Egypt, certainly, but at least to me, her eyes remembered Spain and reflected five hundred years of exile. She had inherited the Sephardic sadness of those centuries and yet retained—against all experience—an optimism I came to see was a belief in the redemptive power of physical passion. In the act of love, her exile fell away and Miriam entered her own true country.*

Similarly, a line like the last one, which would seem overbaked and excessively "theatrical" outside the perfumed claustrophobia of the harem, makes perfect sense given the (confining) circumstances. The narrator has an affair with Miriam.

> *She purred, a sound she often made and one that always caused me to shiver in anticipation as she again rolled into my arms. She was my Sephardic cat and she accepted intrigue as the normal order of things, not unlike the weather. Perhaps Farouk was right. To Hell with Thucydides, to Hell with history. This was why young men leave home. I was in Egypt, in a languid sun-drenched room in the harem of the Palace, in the arms of a woman who knew more about love than I did.*

Their lovemaking takes place not at night, but during the long languid Egyptian afternoons.

> *When we lay in her bed, which was made of bentwood and curved at the foot like the prow of a boat, I sometimes felt myself floating up to the whitewashed ceiling and watching the two of us wrapped together below. It was a sort of vertigo that I knew wasn't real, but was still every bit as vivid as the lovemaking itself, the reality of which I did not question. Miriam knew it, perhaps even caused it. To signal her awareness of my airy state, she might touch me gently or let her hair, which moments earlier had been pinned in a chignon, graze across my face. The personality I had brought to Egypt was breaking off in little chunks, like melting ice.*

The man, the woman, the people, the culture, the affair, the passage of life—it all rushes by like the scenery of modern life, with only an occasional roadside sign to mark the time. When the scenery isn't all that engaging, its *passing by* arrests our attention and we become aware of the processes churning inside us. That leads us (sooner or later) to the erotic corners of our psyche.

Look again at how time, place, setting furniture, scenery, clothing—even anatomy—serve to dredge up the sensual character of the moment. It's another place and another time—*The Danish Girl*, by David Ebershoff, takes us back to the Paris of the 1970s—but with a sensitivity to the quickening flow of the human landscape that is as clear a fingerprint of late twentieth century America as one is likely to find.

Enid lifted one of the black shades in the little room. Behind the smudged glass was a girl in a leotard and black stockings, one foot on a bentwood chair. She was dancing, although there was no music. Peering out of another little window was the face of a man, his oily nose pressed white to the glass. His breath left a stain of fog. The girl seemed aware of Einar and the other man; before she'd yank off a bit of clothing she would look around, although not directly at their flat-nosed faces and dip her chin.

She peeled a pair of gloves similar to Lili's off the fleshy pipe of her arm. The girl was not pretty: black hair electric and dry, a horse's jaw, hips too wide and stomach too narrow. But there was something lovely in her modesty, Einar thought; in the way she neatly draped her gloves and then her leotard and finally her stockings over the back of the bentwood chair, as if she knew she would need them again.

Soon she was naked except for her shoes. She started to dance more energetically, her toes pointing, her hands held out. She threw her head back, exposing her white-blue trachea pressing against her skin.

So now, bear with me and let's have a little fun (on the way to driving to a point). See if you can match the sentences with the young women writer. First the sentences:

1. *"Taking another sip of bourbon, I put on the plastic gloves and began parting my hair at the roots."*

2. *"The first time I had sex with a man for money, it was September—still like summer, but the heat in the motel room was on and it seemed to coat my throat with dust."*

3. *"'Call it fucking,' said her Valium-giddy sister, Allison, in the dressing room beforehand."*

4. *"Smoke has as many different scents as skin."*

5. *"Her body was slender, almost starved, giving her delicate beauty the strange arrested sensuality of unsatisfied want."*

Now the writers:

A. Mary Gaitskill
B. Laura Kasischke

C. June Spence
D. Darcey Steinke
E. Rene Steinke

The answers are forthcoming.

IN THE INTRODUCTION TO MY FIRST COLLECTION OF CONTEMPORARY American erotica, *The Good Parts,* I wrote that "with an astounding variety of viewpoints and a rich diversity of styles, contemporary women writers have not just revitalized but totally reinvented erotic fiction." I didn't know the half of it. The last decade of the twentieth century gave us whole new sexual vocabularies. For one, there was the technological revolution. At the end of 1999 it was estimated that between seventeen and thirty million people log on to a sex site every day. Hence the new vocabulary of the Internet: cybersex, cyberkink, cyberporn, cyberslut, cyberpredator, as well as phrases like virtual bondage, S & M chatroom, and "one-handed" typing. Other additions to the language include riot girls, lipstick lesbians, born-again virgins, post-punk-irony girl, and the "new modesty" to name just five.

When you look at recent American fiction, it's readily apparent that it is women writers, much more than their male counterparts, who are intent on describing the brave new millennial worlds of contemporary erotica. It is women who are testing the limits, women who are pushing the boundaries, women who are most particularly staking out new territory when it comes to the dark side of sexuality—those deep dreams of the human psyche where danger dates desire. These women expand upon the most American of traits, voyeuristic obsession, darting from exterior to interior details and back again. They exhibit their facility for lushness of setting as well as lushness of psychology. And often they're doing it right from the very first line. Here are five of the best beginnings (which contain the answers to the quiz).

First, the opening paragraph of the short story "Words for What She Wanted" by June Spence:

> *Talking was such a poor substitute for sex, Edwina was starting to think, though she did either with what appeared to be grace and aplomb, the way she sang at her sister Allison's wedding and waiting with her arthritic father. "Truly radiant," her father said of both his daughters that day. "Call it fucking," said her Valium-giddy sister, Allison, in the dressing room beforehand. "That's what it is." Edwina cringed at the rude smack of the word, a sound made at even the thought of it, and inwardly revised. She preferred abandon or reverie as much for their lurid paperback quality as their toppling syllables. She was imperious about language but humble in other respects. "It doesn't take much to get me lost," she said when they were heading from the church to the reception hall, and handed her map over to the best man. She was perhaps overly solicitous of the maid of honor, who was embarrassed at being chosen over the bride's own sister. But that was how Edwina was.*

The reader's curiosity is immediately piqued by what Spence chooses to reveal about Edwina, Allison, and their father.

Why does Edwina cringe at the word "fucking" if she does it "with what appeared to be grace and aplomb"?

Why is she "imperious about language but humble in other respects"?

Why is Allison giddy with Valium on her wedding day? And what does it say about their father that he feels the need to call both daughters "truly radiant." We read on, eager to know.

GREAT BEGINNING NUMBER 2 COMES FROM MARY GAITSKILL. NOT only is she one of our best writers, young or old, she's also a one-woman antidote to pseudo-hip minimalism. No spare, hardly-there, wannabe-chic explorations of emptiness. No bare-bones bullshit. She's a maximalist and always gives the reader highly detailed, fully realized depictions of contemporary life that appeal to all five senses as well as the brain. This is how she starts her short story "The Dentist":

> *In Jill's neighborhood there was a giant billboard advertisement of a perfume called Obsession. It was mounted over the chain grocery store at which she shopped, and so she glanced at it several times a week. It was a close-up black and white photograph of an exquisite girl with the fingers of one hand pressed against her own lips. Her eyes were fixated, wounded, deprived. At the same time, her eyes were flat. Her body was slender, almost starved, giving her delicate beauty the strange, arrested sensuality of unsatisfied want. But her fleshy lips and enormous eyes were sumptuously, even grossly abundant. The photograph loomed over the toiling shoppers like a totem of sexualized pathology, a vision of feeling and unfeeling chafing together. It was a picture made for people who can't bear to feel*

> *and yet still need to feel. It was a picture by people sophisticated enough to fetishize their disability publicly. It was a very good advertisement for a product called Obsession.*

This is vintage Gaitskill. "Arrested sensuality of unsatisfied want" joining with "fleshy . . . sumptuously . . . abundant . . . a totem of sexualized pathology" and "people sophisticated enough to fetishize their disability publicly." In one paragraph she says more about today's relationship between advertising, desire, money, and women's bodies than dozens of articles or books on the subject. This paragraph should be on anybody's list of great starts to good stories.

Now three novelists:

> *Was it the bourbon or the dye fumes that made the pink walls quiver like vaginal lips? And acidy scent ribboned the pawed tub, fingered up the shower curtain. My vision was liquid and various as a Lava lamp. In the mirror I saw the scar from the blackberry bramble that caught my chin and scratched a hairline curve to my forehead. It was hardly noticeable, but left the impression that my face was cracked. Taking another sip of bourbon, I put on the plastic gloves and began parting my hair at the roots. As the dye snaked out there was a faint sucking sound, like soil pulling water, and I wondered: if I were brave enough to slit my wrists would I bother to dye my hair?*

This is Darcey Steinke's *Suicide Blonde*. The book has been called "a disturbing poisonous fable" (true) and "the diary of a death wish" (also true). But what strikes me about it is the way that Steinke's writing is full of the tangible stuff of life. Take the above paragraph. A Lava lamp, a blackberry bramble, bourbon, plastic gloves, and vaginal lips all together in one very arresting and very original version of the world. Steinke does this throughout the novel. Live chickens in poultry-shop cages, rubber penises with feet, scallop shells in neat array, and warm Mexican rain all coexist. The effect is that whatever sexual deprivation she describes, it seems to be just another of part of the stuff of life. Life is full of things, her narrator seems to saying. There is sadistic anal sex just as there is rain on a rose garden. There are sperm stains just as there is the reassuring bubbling of fish tanks. There is a hand (her hand) closely examined the morning after it jerks off a total stranger and there is the welcoming warm green light of a rental car's dashboard. It's all part of the same world.

LAURA KASISCHKE BEGINS HER NOVEL *Suspicious River* with another take-no-prisoners line:

> *The first time I had sex with a man for money, it was September—still like summer, but the heat in the motel room was on and it seemed to coat my throat with dust. The man was dull, small-eyed, no taller than myself, but he seemed afraid. He wouldn't look at me. When I asked him what he wanted to do, he said, "That's your job."*
>
> *There was a powdery film between us, the glare of the one*

lamp on the nightstand making haze of the artificial heat. I could see my own image through the haze, above the dresser, reflected in a mirror the length and width of a coffin—a silver one, lined with mercury and sterling, a stainless steel table in an operating room, or morgue, propped up against a wall.

That was my own body floating in that mirror, I thought, reflected in sharp triangles of light. My body in a closet of pure flat space, like a piece of bent sheet metal abandoned on a beach.

From the outset, Kasischke's narrator is linking sex and death. The mirror is the length and width of a silver coffin. Or it's a stainless steel table in an operating room or, even worse, a morgue. Her body is not of the earth. It's "floating in that mirror." Or it's been abandoned on a beach. As the story unfolds, we learn that Leila, the protagonist, is desperately trying to make connections between childhood sexual violence, her mother's murder, and her current life as a prostitute in a desperate midwestern small town. Kasischke is an award-winning poet and the book is filled with poetic evocations, often at the disturbing juncture of nature and sex.

It's a canopy of red in the branches over our heads, gold. The light is hennaed. The color of my hair. I feel pretty when he looks through a cool burnish of leaves at me. Two squirrels chase each other through high branches, and the sun pours lavish onto their copper fur. Like my hair, which he touches with the tips of his fingers. I feel beautiful because he wants me, and the river shivers and ripples like a black sheet, a wet velvet dress.

For Leila, nature seems initially to offer some solace, but she is so scarred psychologically that nature often ends up reflecting her preoccupation with death and sexuality: "the river shivers and ripples like a black sheet, a wet velvet dress."

THE FIFTH AND FINAL KNOCKOUT OPENING COMES FROM RENE Steinke's 1999 novel, *The Fires,* which a friend of mine likes to call the last great novel of the century:

Smoke has as many different scents as skin. Part of the pleasure is not knowing what it will be—sulfurous or closer to incense or airier and sweet as I imagine the smell of clouds. Nothing relieves me as much as burning something old, watching it flicker and disappear into air. Dresses dance as they go, lifted as if by some music. A photograph flaps like a wing or a hand waving. Perfumes hiss, then shatter, paper curls, plaster jewels curdle. Once I tried to burn an old toy—a mechanical duck. When I'd found it at the bottom of a drawer, it reminded me of a groggy sunrise Easter service and the hunt for the eggs in the graveyard. After I set the match to its tail, it started walking pitifully on its metal legs, and it knocked around the room singeing the walls and linoleum until it burned down to its metal frame and folded with a crackle and a small battery explosion. It is less dangerous to burn things than to save them.

I'd poured myself six thimble shots of bourbon and walked

> *the edges of the bedroom touching the walls and the windowsills, hoping to work the starry twitches from my legs so they lie still. If I let go, I'd fall off the night that was galloping fast.*

Like Laura Kasischke's Leila, Rene Steinke's Ella has deep emotional scars. But she's also physically scarred from a childhood fire. And like Leila she's desperately trying to come up with answers as she finds herself "entangled in a complicated web of secrets surrounding her father's death, her grandfather's suicide, her aunt's mysterious disappearance, her mother's descent into anorexia and depression." All this could easily become gothic potboiler bilge were in not for Steinke's acute intelligence and her haunting lyricism, which is most evident when she is describing Ella's pyromania.

> *Those flames passed before I could hold them, make them lie down and stroke their grain. They slid through my fingers and trilled into the ceiling. When I caught them in my fist, they evaporated. I wanted to press them into balls I would save in a tin box and take out to roll on my palm and study their color, cut one open to see the roiling interior like an intestine or a heart.*

The answer to our quiz, then is: 1. D; 2. B; 3. C; 4. E; 5. A. What Mary Gaitskill, Laura Kasischke, June Spence, Darcey Steinke, and Rene Steinke illustrate beyond a doubt is this: When it comes to erotica in serious fiction, American writers have lots of new things to say and lots of new ways to say those things. The natural way the erotic has entered the emotional landscape, no more out of place than a garish roadside diner on a drab stretch of thruway, has allowed these writers to explore that most fascinating and mysterious of terrain—us.

Enjoy the collection!

—J. H. Blair
Princeton, June 2000

MARTHA BAER

As Francesca

Martha Baer is executive editor of Hot Wired. *She was founding member of the New York Performance Art Group The V-Girls, and currently lives in San Francisco. Her first novel,* As Francesca, *a hauntingly passionate tale that perfectly captures the allure of anonymous cybersex, is the most inventive and erotic fiction of the e-mail age.*

THIS TIME I WANTED IT IN MY MOUTH. HOW IT HAPPENS THAT LONGings move through your body, shifting from place to place in your being like ancient animals in their deliberate migrations over spans of the globe, over generations, settling in regions from one continent to another to graze and to grow, I'm not in a position to say. Why sometimes the core of my wanting resides in the palms of my hands, the insides of my thighs, or deep up inside me, I am not equipped to explain. And yet the fact of this shifting is unmistakable to me, as real as the most well-researched anthropology. I always knew precisely the spot where my desire was lodged. So that this time, as I sat there awaiting her summons, entirely ignorant of the digital gaffe that had obscured my identity, I knew exactly where my cravings originated and satisfaction belonged. My hands were a pointless detour, a cul-de-sac, even if last time they seemed central. I wanted it in my mouth.

I wanted to taste it. I wanted its saltiness to surprise my tongue. I wanted to know intimately its hardness and softness—that particular tension between the two poles, balanced as purely as a mathematical equation whose solution is sex itself—I wanted to travel its hard and soft surface, wildly attentive, abundantly sure, with the delicate skin of my lips.

I could taste it already. The minute I saw that name, those four little shapes, written as if somewhere emblazoned or as if deeply, materially etched in, I had begun to imagine the shadow of it brushing up against my taste buds and my insanely awakened tongue.

But in all of this sexual extravagance, which, like some enormous libidinal celebration was crowded with fantasies and packed with feeling, there was one thought that was strangely absent: the fact that "Inez," who had been my paramour, who had taken me apart so many times now, bearing down on me with all that oddly loving brutality and making me come again and again, the fact that Inez, who had always been a "her" to me, no longer definitively was, didn't faze me at all. It made not a mark, not a chink, on the great hulking presence of my need. How ludicrous, you might think, that I simply didn't notice the sudden introduction of that part, that member, which she offered to me in our last encounter like a trophy presented amid the furor of the finish line, or, that having noticed it, I just didn't care.

It came down to nothing more than a problem of boredom, of plain old ennui. Because to ponder now, after all this time, the pronoun of her, the shocking possibility of her difference, would really boil down to exploring one elementary question, a question which, when compared with the thrill of what I'd been getting was, with all due respect, impossibly dull: Was it attached?

Was it connected? And if so to what? Was it attached to that little spot on the body we all hold so dear? Was it fixed there permanently, fastened with matter we'd like to call "natural," with skin and sinew, material with which "she" had been born? Or was it, on the other hand, affixed with something unnatural, like nylon, for instance, or rubber, or like leather, something ambiguously in between? One way or another, connected or autonomous, held in place there with his or her hands, the object belonged to an incredible sexual genius, whose sole motive for wielding it was to find my desire and approach the sublime. And in the light of the extraordinary thrill of Inez, the thoroughly overpowering fact of the act, and the fantasy of the object inside me, this series of rudimentary queries seemed intolerably banal. One sentiment quite plainly asserted itself: why bother?

I sat before my monitor glazed over with lust, feeling a wetness, like wishing itself, collect, uncontrollably, in my mouth. My tongue was a muscle with a presence. I was lost in a recollection of that last encounter, the way she'd let me touch it then pushed away my hand, the way she'd convinced me that I could get near it and then lifted me up and turned me around.

As Inez transmuted before me, lost her form, her gender, radically, and reclaimed it anew only to lose it once more, I experienced all this lacking of certainty as a thing in the end I had gained. It was as if I were advancing up a slow, steady incline, gradually approaching the top, and as I got nearer, inching toward the crest, the view of the surrounding landscape expanded. Now, it was true that I lost something by rising, that all the detailed foliage and rocks on the ridge withdrew and were gone, as was the now-distant horizon, but equally, at the very same time, I gained in taking in the scope of things, taking in more and more breadth as I climbed.

Absently, I'd begun loosening my shirt. I was watching for a message at the foot of the screen. Transfixed by the feel of my own mouth from the inside and the memory of wrapping my greedy fingers around her, I'd begun to unbutton my soft cotton blouse. Nothing had happened. For minutes I'd been sitting there passive, staring at the unchanging screen, but no messages had come in.

I was flushed. Next I found myself untucking my shirt from my jeans. What, I wondered, was delaying her? I sat up straight. The longing was rising up through me, as if to escape, like air through the vents, with the loosening of my clothes. Is she ignoring me, I thought, is she teasing? My face grew warmer and a gust of heat seemed to sweep through me. God, I said, perhaps even aloud, whispering, she could torture me like this forever. In the ribbon of commands across the top of the window, I saw the time jolt forward one digit. I knew I would have to plead. It was more vivid than ever how officially I was owned.

But in the moment that I began typing, ready to serve up my little verbal supplication, ready to beg—it was nothing really to begin with, just "Inez, please"—I saw, like a flash of light in my unguarded eyes, the person my words were ascribed to. As if heaving myself out of my daze, I recognized what was happening. No wonder Inez had ignored me, I thought. My plea was ascribed to "Elaine."

Immediately I entered the change-name command. The server sent a response without a lag that came up at the foot of the screen, and though I knew what it would say, I read it over voraciously:

"<Elaine V. Botsch> changes her name to <Francesca>." She would speak to me now, I was certain.

And yet, still I waited. At that point my real name, "Francesca," must have shown plainly at the top of Inez's display—in some darkened room, in some far city—and unless she were truly teasing me, punishing me somehow, or confused, there was no reason why she wouldn't have addressed me. It was already twenty-five past. I was leaning in, my arms and face covered with the ashen glow from my screen. My hands were holding the base of the machine, and all that sensation, so rife in my mouth just moments before, had gone out of me. Something new and strange had occurred, but in my building panic that it might be irreparable, I could barely consider what it was.

Finally I tried writing her again, though I had never, in all these months, been the one to speak first. I wrote out the line and rewrote it, misspelling and deleting, writing back over my scrambled words. "Inez," was all I'd come up with, "I'm ready. Whatever it is you want."

Still, there was nothing. A weird freeze seemed to set in to my bones, as if I'd been unexpectedly caught in the mountains, the sun going down, and my camp snowed in. I was stricken with the sense that I'd already been left by her. With me, the give-and-take, or the taking back, the waiting and the withholding, is like a tunnel. Sucked into a dark and isolated space, the space of blind desire and narrow vision, I am consumed with a longing for the other side. Nothing touches me but the possibility of that other opening. And often, when I feel myself wanting that fiercely, if a fear that the light is unapproachable sets in, I begin to forget myself entirely. Whole portions of my body, my mind, and my character begin to go dim. It is a kind of paralysis of wanting, as if without regular activity my own desire can't live.

Still nothing happened. Short of losing sight completely of the tunnel's distant opening, I felt I had to say more. I added another line, composing it quickly but with fanatic concentration: "Anything," it said. "Inez. I will give you whatever you ask."

Nothing.

"Inez. God. Anything."

I waited.

Finally—the clock at the top of my screen now reading thirty-eight after—with no explanation, she wrote me. She sent it, just a number, a destination, "16." And if I'd ever been willing before in my life, then it must have been such a mild form of it as to belong to another realm, because the willingness I experienced in that instant that night, as I rabidly hit those keys, spelling out "goto 16," bore no resemblance to what I'd ever called eagerness before.

Inez already knew everything: "You want it in your mouth, don't you?" she wrote.

I was mortified by my predictability. But with the mere mention of it, made manifest in those few unambiguous words, my awareness of the now-primary orifice came surging back. Again my mouth was the site of countless decades of deprivation, the place where a new definition for the notion of hunger was now and forever being formed. How is it that, after all these millennia of spoken language, there's no word to stand in for that single particular longing—not "thirst," which is for water, not "loneliness," which is for love—but for the longing, simply, to suck?

"Well?" she said. She wanted me to say it, to tell her exactly how the craving felt.

I couldn't answer. I had no idea what to do next.

"Then get on your knees," she said. "Now." She waited, dropped to a new line. "Get down."

At that point, for me, it was almost as if it were already over. It was as if the whole thing, the arousal and the climax, had grown so perfectly vivid that it already existed, complete and autonomous, inside me. It had reached such a point of reality in my mind, like a disease fully blown, that there was no reason to do anything but watch it grow. And what was most odd of all was that Inez seemed to know this, or perhaps she had simply changed her mood, because what she did next was distinctly different from the ways she'd behaved before. It was not simply a variation. It was different in pace, in purpose, in tone. Inez, for the first time in all our violently passionate electronic encounters, had become gentle.

"Yes," she said, "baby. I know that you want it." The endearment was glaringly new. At first I couldn't tell if there was contempt in it or sarcasm.

But there was none. "You want it, I know, I can tell," she continued. "It's OK, I'll take care of you." She paused. "Tip back your head, sweetheart, and obey me."

And I did, of course. I obeyed her. I leaned back in my chair.

She said, "I'm taking your gorgeous face in my hands. It's burning."

Just like that, with that care and coolness, she kept talking. I read it as if it were destiny. Whatever she said, it didn't matter, really, because I felt as if I'd already taken it in. Her words were as close to me, as intimate and knowable, as the feel of my very own skin.

"Your face is hot, Francesca. Your neck is long. Your mouth is opening, and I'm running my hands through your hair."

I was swaying. Everything was brilliantly, crystally clear. There was only the barely audible question floating in and out of my mind as to whether I'd come now or after.

"OK," she said. "Now take it."

And at that moment, everything, the room and the screen and my own reading, my deciphering of the words and understanding, my very thinking and absorbing, was all one immense and spectacular metaphor for the act of penetration.

RUSSELL BANKS

Affliction

Russell Banks is the author of numerous critically acclaimed works of fiction, including Continental Drift, Affliction, *and* The Sweet Hereafter. *More than any other writer, he has raised the tradition of small-town American realism to a high art.*

HE MOVED CLOSER TO HER, AND SHE STOPPED TWIRLING HER LEG in the air and looked up at him. Reaching out with one hand, he brushed her chin with his fingertips, then lowered himself down next to her and laid his head on her lap, facing away from her toward the shabby couch and across the cluttered room to the darkened window beyond. The room looked to him exactly as it had when he had lived here with Lillian twenty years before, and he had knelt beside her and had placed his head in her lap, and looking away from her, so that she could not see the tears in his eyes, he had begged her to forgive him. Hettie stroked his head, as if he were a troubled child, and he set the bottle of beer on the floor and reached around her legs with his arms and held her tightly.

"Wade," she said. "No."

"When we lived here," he said in a low voice, "it was mostly good. There were some bad times, but it was mostly good. Wasn't it?"

"Wade, that was a long time ago. Like, things change, Wade."

"No. Some things stay the same your whole life. The best things that happened to you, and the worst, they stay with you your whole life. When we lived here, when we were kids just starting out, that was the best thing. I know that. I can still feel that, in spite of everything else that has happened to us."

"Wade," Hettie said, her voice almost a whisper. "Why did you come over here tonight?"

He was silent for a few seconds, and then he said, "Will you let me make love to you?" He released her and sat back on his heels and looked up at her face, which was filled with confusion and fear, although he did not see that. He said, "Just this one time, here, in this place. In the dark, with the lights out, and you can be Lillian, and I'll be whoever you want. I'll be Jack, if you want. Just this one time."

"I can't, Wade. I'm scared. No kidding, really. I'm scared of this. You should go."

"In the dark I can call you Lillian, and you can call me Jack. And it will only happen this one time. I need to do that. Lillian."

"Please. Please don't call me Lillian." Her eyes welled up, and tears broke across her cheeks. "You're scaring me."

Wade reached up and touched her hair at the bottom of her long slender neck. "You look nice with your hair cut short like that," he said, and he reached beyond her to the light switch on the wall and doused the overhead light, a bulb hidden in a Chinese paper shade, dropping the room into darkness, with only the lamp in the bedroom showing now, casting a long plank of light into the room, so that they could see the shape of each other's bodies but could not make out the face. And he did look like Jack to her at that moment, kneeling next to her, one hand on her thigh, the other on her shoulder, his fingertips brushing her throat. He said, "I wonder what your hair smells like now. If it smells the same as it used to when I kissed you and we made love."

She was shaking; her heart was pounding and the blood roared in her ears.

"Lillian," he said. "Say my name. Say it."

"This scares me. Don't."

"I want you to say my name. Jack. Say it."

"I'm afraid. I really am."

"Lillian."

She whispered his name. "Jack."

He touched her lips with the tips of his fingers. "Say it again."

"Jack."

He took her hand and placed her fingers across his lips, and he said, "Lillian."

He stood slowly and said, "Wait here," and he walked into the bedroom, crossed to the bedside table and put out the light. Then he quickly returned through the darkness to stand behind her.

She said, "This scares me a whole lot. We shouldn't do this."

"It's all right. We're not who we are. I'm Jack, and you're Lillian." He reached down and placed his hands on her shoulders. He let his hands slide to her breasts and gently hold them, and she laid her head back against him, her breath coming rapidly now, as he moved his hands over her breasts, her nipples hardening, her hands on his, pressing them against her. Then he was kissing her neck, her ears, her cheeks and her lips, and she was kissing him back, and they were standing in the room holding tightly to one another, and in seconds they were moving through the darkness to the bedroom.

She said to me, "I knew it was wrong, but it isn't like I was married to Jack or anything. And things had been pretty bad between him and me lately anyway, Jack and me, since that hunting accident he was involved with. I guess I was mad at him. And I liked Wade, you know, he was like an old friend, ever since I was a kid, and he had always been real sweet to me, and he seemed so sad and all. I really felt sorry for him. And it was like just this one time. I had never been what you'd call attracted to Wade, but this one night, it was different. And making me call him Jack like that, and him calling me Lillian, it was strange, like being real high, and it kind of took me over, you know?"

Wade undressed her in the darkness, and then he took off his own clothes and moved onto her, gently kissing her with his damaged mouth, drawing her warm breath into him, gulping it down. He lifted himself up on his arms, and she opened to him like a flower, and he entered her, easily, with excruciating slowness, until he was all the way in, and he felt huge to himself, as if he had gone all the way up into her chest and were touching Lillian's heart.

FREDERICK BARTHELME

Painted Desert

Frederick Barthelme is the author of three short-story collections and seven novels, including The Brothers *and* Painted Desert, *from which this exhilarating and quintessentially American excerpt is taken. He teaches writing at the University of Southern Mississippi, where he also edits* The Mississippi Review.

THE DESERT WASN'T FLAT, BUT IT WAS PLENTY EMPTY. THE BIG Town Car was the only thing on the highway at that time of the morning. We got some miles in, crossing the Hopi Indian reservation, the car washing along the two-lane at fifty-five miles an hour—Jen was going easy. After a time she slowed up and stopped at a spot where a red dirt lane cut north off the highway, straight into the desert. It wasn't a real road at all, just some packed ground where other cars had obviously turned in. We were parked there in the middle of the highway when Jen opened her car door, got out, and stood up on the sill, looking into the desert. "I'm going here," she finally said.

I was out of the car too, standing in the road. There was nobody as far as the eye could see in front of us or behind us on the highway, no lights, nothing but a few insistent stars and the craggy silhouettes of dark desert rock against a still-sleepy sky. I couldn't see anything anywhere. Jen was walking around kicking up dust on the shoulder of the road. The dirt-covered Lincoln was idling there.

"Straight across, huh?" I said.

"It'll come out somewhere," she said.

"I guess," I said.

So we got back in Mike's car and she swung us into the dirt road and in a few minutes we were cutting across open land. Sometimes there was a road under us, sometimes tracks, sometimes just uncluttered ground.

As the darkness evaporated and lifted off the desert floor, the land around us turned into a bigger-than-life topographical map, its colors eerie and surprising as the sun began to brighten the horizon from below. I felt light-headed to finally be off L.A., to be out in the country in this way we'd never planned.

After forty minutes of gliding up the desert, I reached in back for the little TV and said, "I'll try to get something."

Jen caught my hand and stopped me. "Do try the radio," she said. Then she hit the gas hard, picking up speed. I saw it cross eighty.

I punched the Seek button a few times, and the tuner caught a preacher, a sports talk show, finally a news station. The announcer was talking about snakes, how there were too many snakes, and how they were having an impact on the tourist business. He called it a rain of snakes.

"I want to marry you when we get home," Jen said. "Regular married. Just like everybody."

"You do?"

"Is it a deal?"

I punched the little chrome button to drop my window, then stuck my arm straight out into the buffeting wind, flying my hand the way I'd done as a kid. "I guess it's a deal for me," I said.

She waved at the radio and said, "Find some music."

"What do you want?" I punched the Seek button again, watching the numbers flip by.

"Swing," she said. "Western swing."

I kept hitting the button, but I couldn't find anything that made sense to listen to, so I left it on Autoseek—ten seconds of every station. For a minute all I could think of was what we must look like from the sky, the black Lincoln, the two splintered headlights shooting out into nothing, the two taillights glowing red tracers behind us, the big flat space everywhere and all this dust swelling around us like a land-speed-record attempt. We rocketed across that desert sand.

LAUREN BELFER

City of Light

Lauren Belfer grew up in Buffalo, New York, and received her MFA in fiction from Columbia University in New York City. City of Light, *her debut novel, is set in the confident and booming Buffalo of 1901 when it was the eighth most populous city in America—the world's greatest port, exceeded only by London, Liverpool, Hamburg, New York, and Chicago in total tonnage. It is a striking work of historical imagination. She lives in Manhattan with her husband and son.*

I WAS IN AN UNLIT ENTRYWAY.

"Come along then," I heard the president say from a room at the end of the entry gallery, and I walked toward his voice.

The suite's opulent sitting room was decorated with heavy curtains and hand-painted wallpaper, feathery forest scenes in the style of Fragonard. The former president looked up from a newspaper. He had changed, taking off his shoes and his jacket and tie. He wore a silk paisley dressing gown over his trousers and open shirt. This surprised me. But then I realized he would want to relax after his day's full schedule. There was a glass of brandy on the well-polished table beside him. He smoked a cigar. The night was warm and humid. The air in the room was oppressive. I felt pressure in my chest from breathing the cigar smoke. Not knowing what else to do, I stayed near the door.

"Well," he said, looking me up and down, evaluating me. From the look that came into his face, he seemed to relish what he saw. "Good evening." He stretched out the words meaningfully—although for what meaning I had no idea. Stubbing out the cigar in the crystal ashtray, he got up, lumbering, and padded toward me across the thick carpet, the silk of his dressing gown rustling.

I stepped back, to the wall beside the door.

"You're certainly a beauty," he said.

"Oh. Thank you." I flushed in embarrassment. I felt pleased by the compliment but startled that he would notice my appearance. I still didn't understand. My bewilderment seemed to please him.

"First-timer, are we?" he asked, smiling. I didn't know what he meant. I was unprepared when he took my shoulders and pulled me close and kissed me, filling my mouth with the acrid taste of cigars. There was a line of perspiration along the top of his mustache, and it dampened my cheeks.

I tried to push him away. "What are you doing?" I choked.

But my pushing only made him tighten his grip on my shoulders. "Playful, are we?" he asked, not displeased.

"I'd better go," I blurted. "This isn't—I didn't—I'd better go." He pressed me hard against the wall. He was big, so big—Big Steve, his friends had called him when he was young—and I struggled but couldn't escape. His body surrounded me like a supple barrier, present wherever I turned.

"What lovely eyes you have." Holding my chin, he moved my head slightly back and forth. "Dark blue, eh?"

I couldn't respond.

He gazed at me indulgently. "Now, now, my dear. Don't be like that." He touched his forehead against mine, rubbing for a moment. "And besides, wouldn't you like to know what it's like? What the poets sing about?" He nuzzled my neck, whispering in limpid tones. "Haven't you ever wondered?" He kissed along the line where my cheek met my hair. "Any girl as pretty as you deserves to know everything life can offer, eh?"

"Please. Let me go," I begged.

He patted my hair. "Go where?" His touch was gentle. "Mmmm? Where exactly is it that you want to go?" His voice was tender. "Do you want to go running down the hall and into the lobby where everyone will see you? It's very late, for a young lady like yourself to be out alone. And in a hotel, of all places." He rubbed his private self against my leg. "What would the reporters think? And I'm sure the reporters are still there—they always keep a close eye on me when I travel. The local reporters, I mean. The ones who'd have no trouble determining your identity." I felt myself about to cry. Tears caught in my throat.

"And even if you escape the lobby unscathed, how will you get home?" He rubbed his private self harder, adjusting his body so that his bulky middle didn't interfere. "How would you find a hansom driver who wouldn't talk? Or will you walk home, do you think, miles and miles through the streets?" Again I struggled against him, and he grabbed my wrists, hard. "No, no. You stay now, and I'll make sure you get home safely. And secretly." Letting go of my wrists, he put his arms around me and pulled me tighter against him. His breath was warm upon my ear. "And really, my dear"—now his forearms pressed against my back to hold me while his fingers pulled down my hair—"I think it'll do you good. No one will ever know. I promise you. You'll never be put to shame. It's too late to change your mind, anyway." He rubbed harder, his legs entrapping me. "Too late."

And he was right. How could I get home without his help? Without his help, I would be compromised beyond repair. I would lose my job and I would never find another—not teaching, that is. Any dream I'd ever had would be over. I hated myself for my ignorance. All of this was my fault: I hadn't known the code, I hadn't understood the subtext of his words. It was too late now, to go back. His promise of secrecy was all I could rely on to protect me.

I stopped fighting him. I became impassive, like a small, trapped animal.

"So." In his pleasure he lengthened the word. He kissed away a tear upon my eyelid. "Good girl." Nonetheless, when he pressed his lips to mine, pushing his tongue against my teeth, instinctively I turned away, his saliva leaving a band across my cheek. Laughing he caught my face in the palm of his hand. "Still shy?" He tapped my nose with one tender fingertip. "No need to be shy with me."

He guided me to the bedroom. When my footsteps became reluctant, he gripped my wrist and twisted my arm behind me—laughing still, as if it were a game, my resistance a show that pleased him more and more. The bedside lamp was lit. The bed had a brocaded canopy.

It wasn't necessary for me to undress completely, that would take too much time, he said. With hurried fingers, he fumbled with the buttons of my dress, letting the silk fall to the floor as he pulled at my underclothes. The petticoats and the corset stayed on. He took off his trousers and undergarments, taking the time to fold them over a chair. He left on his shirt and dressing gown. Then he folded down the bedspread, keeping it even and neat. He lay upon his back and smiled at me encouragingly. But when I didn't join him, he sat up suddenly and grabbed me. "None of that now," he said, his smile gone—but gone only for an instant. In a tone that could only be described as loving, he added, "It's natural to feel nervous the first time. But it won't be so bad."

He moved me into position atop his legs. He put my hands around his private self, his hands over mine. He made my hands rub him, up and down.

"There you go, there you go," he said, his voice gentle, his grip crippling. Up and down, up and down, his hands over mine. Abruptly he placed his hands behind my head and pushed my head down—I didn't know what he wanted, didn't even know what he was thinking. In confusion I glanced at his half-closed eyes. He grunted in response. He shifted, pulling my body into position over him and pressing me down upon him. There was resistance, beyond my control, my body not opening to him. I had no notion what to do. He was displeased. His smile turned to a grimace. He used his spit to ease his way, gripping my hips and moving me to his exact pleasure.

I wondered then, as he pressed inside me, more than hurting me, *this* is the great and hidden knowledge of life? *This?* This is what men and women have whispered about and created elaborate rituals to sanctify? Is this how it is with your wife, Frances, she who came to you as innocent as I, she who claims publicly to adore you? Is this what she adores? Your stomach like a rubbery cushion, propping her up? Or are you different with her? Is it possible to be different?

I stared at the brocaded canopy. I didn't know how long it would take. But suddenly he gave a self-satisfied sigh, and it was over. He rested, smirking. Sweat glistened on his forehead. I didn't move.

After a few minutes, the president instructed me to leave. He was finished. Besides, he didn't want to keep his assistant secretary, who would take me home, up late when they had another busy day tomorrow. "And we can't rely on poor Gilder to get you home," he added. "He's undoubtedly off somewhere resting his nerves." The president chuckled as if this were a very good joke.

Delicately, he pushed me off him. When I stood, the offal of his body flowed down my thighs. I dared not make a show of wiping it away. The smell of it made me gag. I pressed the back of my hand against my face to block the smell. I dressed as quickly as I could, my fingers shaking. This time he didn't help me.

An overly thin young man with ruddy cheeks and glasses waited outside the suite. The assistant secretary. Without looking at me, he led me to a carriage that had pulled in close to the hotel's back door. For the sake of anonymity, the carriage dropped me at the deserted park, leaving me not far from the lake where one day Karl Speyer would drown. From there I walked home through deserted streets, trying to steel myself against tears. Tears would do me no good now. Besides, I had saved myself: I should be proud, I told myself over and over, defending myself against despair, fighting off self-pity. I had saved myself. I gripped my shawl across my chest as if it could protect me.

In those days, I lived on the top floor of a house on the far side of Elmwood Avenue. My landlady was an elderly woman of genteel poverty; my rent allowed her to maintain her home. Her hearing was such that she never noticed my late-night footsteps.

THOMAS BELLER

"Life Under Optimum Conditions"

Thomas Beller grew up in New York City, where he now lives. He attended Vassar College and received an MFA from the Columbia Writers' Program. His short stories and articles have appeared in The New Yorker, Mademoiselle, Ploughshares, Epoch, *and* Best American Short Stories 1992, *among others. He is one of the founding editors of the literary magazine* Open City. *His first collection,* Seduction Theory, *was both a critical and commercial success.*

WHAT HAD STARTED AS A WONDERFUL ADVENTURE FULL OF ROMANtic possibilities had suddenly become something entirely different. Earlier during the ride the crisp autumn air and unfiltered sunlight had made her think of chestnuts, the smell of burning leaves, and warm cuddling under a thick down comforter. Now it evoked memories of old smelly pencils and Halloween. That particular holiday—only a week away—had once been her favorite, but recently it had taken on an ominous quality, particularly starting the previous year.

She had just moved into a new apartment and had asked the neighbors if children with bags would be coming by. They said yes, a few. She dutifully went out and bought nice candies in small quantities. In the early part of the evening she anticipated the arrival of the small bag bearers with some dread, resenting the imposition. But after a little while she started to enjoy the idea and turned off the lights to create a heightened effect in her apartment; she even regretted not buying a plastic jack-o'-lantern to put the candies in. The night wore on and she sat in the dark listening to her radio. Not a single child came by. At the time she just thought it was eerie, but the next morning she woke feeling like she had suffered a personal rejection.

They pulled into the Beekman Arms parking lot. The first thing she saw was an abnormally large and glowering pumpkin leering out at her from the office window. The expression carved on its face was like that of an obnoxious man who had just seen down her shirt after she bent to pick something up.

"Well," said Michael, his voice raspy from not having spoken in a while, "we're here." He was trying to sound cheerful.

Repenting, she thought. How pathetic.

"Yes, it would appear that way," she said.

They went inside and she registered while he watched. A bellman took them to their room, opening the door for them and turning on the lights. Inside was a four-poster bed, a couch, a fireplace, an elegant glass bottle filled with brandy on the mantel, two snifters by its side. There was plush brown carpet.

It looked seedy and illicit, she thought. She walked into the bathroom without saying a word, and stared at herself glumly in the mirror, looking at the tiny crow's-feet developing around her eyes.

Michael surveyed the room. The bedroom seemed like a sexual obstacle course. It was brimming with possibilities, starting with the fact that it was an empty hotel room at his disposal, and embellished by the couch, the carpet, and especially the grand and voluptuous bed: everything about the place seemed to expect sexual athleticism and experimentation. The room was a blank sheet of paper inviting him to scribble on it, but he had forgotten his crayon. While Jane was in the bathroom he sat gloomily on the edge of the bed and stared at the logs in the dark lifeless fireplace.

They went to dinner in silence. The Beekman Arms restaurant, highly recommended, was suffused in warm atmosphere and busy cheer. It smelled like baked apples and steak. George Washington had once stayed there apparently, on his way to somewhere else. The enormous front door creaked open slowly and smoothly when he pulled on its latch, letting Jane in first.

When they were seated he ordered a bottle of wine after glancing over the wine list, his eyes sticking to the thin column of numbers on the right, since the wider columns of names and dates next to it meant nothing to him. He ordered the second-cheapest one.

Jane was looking around the room. Everyone, she thought, seemed in good spirits. There were happy families, suave middle-aged couples up from the city, and some slightly more earthy types in plaid or flannel of some kind who lived in the area and were pleased to be casually exuding authenticity amidst all these tourists. And there were quite a few lovers, all of whom, she imagined, must be happier than they were just then.

"Do you think you would ever like to live somewhere besides New York?" he asked. "Like in the country?"

"I feel that way nearly all the time," she said.

"Being here makes me feel that way. There's something about the air . . ." He trailed off because she gave him a funny look. "What?" he said.

"Nothing," she replied, looking at the menu.

"Do you think I'm being silly by making dumb small talk?"

She shrugged.

"It is a little ridiculous. I mean, it's not what we usually talk about. But then again we don't usually drive into the country and stay at a hotel."

"Do you want to go back?" she said.

"No! God no." He seemed genuinely alarmed at the idea. "It's just weird."

"Well," she said, "if you think about it there are a lot of things we haven't done together. For all the time we've spent together we still don't really know each other that well."

He thought about this for a moment, a little hurt. "I think we know each other pretty well. Unless there are some deep dark secrets you haven't told me about." She didn't reply. "Are there any deep dark secrets you haven't told me about?"

"I don't know," she said casually, while inspecting the menu. "Probably. Do you have any you haven't told me about?" She didn't look up while asking the question; that would have implied too much interest in the answer.

"I don't know," he said. "Probably."

The wine arrived. Michael knew nothing about wine except for the particular ritual of tasting it when it arrived, which he had observed his father do many times. The waiter poured a little into his glass and Michael commenced his act: after swirling it in his glass, sniffing it, and sipping it pensively with his chin slightly raised, he turned to the waiter and gave a polite nod. As the waiter poured their wine it occurred to Michael for the first time that it might have been an act for his father also. The thought displeased him immensely.

WITHOUT THEIR HAVING TO SAY ANYTHING SPECIFIC, THEIR MANNER softened toward each other over the course of dinner, and by the time they made their way back to their room they were holding hands. After one glass of wine, Michael had decided the situation called for something stronger and he began to drink scotch, saying that the advent of the cooler weather was perfect scotch season. He had several. She finished the wine by herself. So the walk to the room was a little unsteady. And in spite of everything, they made love, or at least engaged in something similar.

The event lived up to his greatest fears: everything seemed a little forced, a little unnatural. The room itself—its props and its atmosphere and its ghosts of past good sex—seemed to goad him into all kinds of unlikely things.

She was amused at this unexpected burst of energy and went along with it, a little puzzled. It became a sexual scavenger hunt: do it lying on the bed, do it with her sitting on the bed while he stood on the floor, do it on the floor next to the fireplace (unlit), and do it in a particularly athletic position halfway between the couch and floor. Then the flowerpot on the coffee table got knocked over and spilled on the carpet and he started to feel silly.

What was left of his erection went away and she said, trying not to sound too discouraging, "Why are we doing this?" and he said, "I don't know," and laughed.

They lit the fire and got under the covers with the lights out.

AIMEE BENDER

The Girl in the Flammable Skirt

Aimee Bender received her MFA in creative writing from the University of California, Irvine. The Girl in the Flammable Skirt, *her first short-story collection from which this excerpt is taken, was a* New York Times *Notable Book of 1998. Her first novel,* An Invisible Sign of My Own, *was published to strong reviews in 2000. She lives in Los Angeles.*

IT IS QUIET IN THE REST OF THE LIBRARY.

Inside the back room, the woman has crawled out from underneath the man. Now fuck me like a dog she tells him. She grips a pillow in her fists and he breathes behind her, hot air down her back which is starting to sweat and slip on his stomach. She doesn't want him to see her face because it is blowing up inside, red and furious, and she's grimacing at the pale white wall which is cool when she puts her hand on it to help her push back into him, get his dick to fill up her body until there's nothing left of her inside: just dick.

The woman is a librarian and today her father has died. She got a phone call from her weeping mother in the morning, threw up and then dressed for work. Sitting at her desk with her back very straight, she asks the young man very politely, the one who always comes into the library to check out bestsellers, asks him when it was he last got laid. He lets out a weird sound and she says shhh, this is a library. She has her hair back and the glasses on but everyone has a librarian fantasy, and she is truly a babe beneath.

I have a fantasy, he says, of a librarian.

She smiles at him but asks her original question again. She doesn't want someone brand new to the business but neither is she looking for a goddamn gigolo. This is an important fuck for her. He tells her it's been a few months and looks sheepish but honest and then hopeful. She says great and tells him there's a back room with a couch for people who get dizzy or sick in the library (which happens surprisingly often), and could he meet her there in five minutes? He nods, he's already telling his friends about this in a monologue in his head. He has green eyes and no wrinkles yet.

They meet in the back and she pulls the shade down on the little window. This is the sex that she wishes would split her open and murder her because she can't deal with a dead father; she's wished him dead so many times that now it's hard to tell the difference between fantasy and reality. Is it true? He's really gone? She didn't really want him to die, that is not what she meant when she faced him and imagined knives sticking into his body. This is not what she meant, for him to actually die. She wonders if she invented the phone call, but she remembers the way her mother's voice kept climbing up and up, and it's so real and true she can't bear it and wants to go fuck someone else. The man is tired now but grinning like he can't believe it. He's figuring when he can be there next, but she's sure she'll never want him again. Her hair is down and glasses off and clothes on the floor and she's the fucked librarian and he's looking at her with this look of adoration. She squeezes his wrist and then concentrates on putting herself back together. In ten minutes, she's at the front desk again, telling a youngster about a swell book on aisle ten, and unless you leaned forward to smell her, you'd never know.

There is a mural on the curved ceiling of the library of fairies dancing. Their arms are interwoven, hair loose from the wind. Since people look at the ceiling fairly often when they're at the library, it is a well-known mural. The librarian tilts her head back to take a deep breath. One of the fairies is missing a mouth. It has burned off from the glare of the sunlight, and she is staring at her fairy friends with a purple-eyed look of muteness. The librarian does not like to see this, and looks down to survey the population of her library instead.

She is amazed as she glances around to see how many attractive men there are that day. They are everywhere: leaning over the wood tables, straight-backed in the aisles, men flipping pages with nice hands. The librarian, on this day, the day of her father's death, is overwhelmed by an appetite she has never felt before and she waits for another one of them to approach her desk.

It takes five minutes.

This one is a businessman with a vest. He is asking her about a book on fishing when she propositions him. His face lights up, the young boy comes clean and clear through his eyes, that librarian he knew when he was seven. She had round calves and a low voice.

She has him back in the room; he makes one tentative step forward and then he's on her like Wall Street rain, his suit in a pile on the floor in a full bucket, her dress unbuttoned down, down, one by one until she's naked and the sweat is pooling in her back again. She obliterates herself and then buttons up. This man too wants to see her again, he might want to marry her, he's thinking, but she smiles without teeth and says, man, this is a one-shot deal. Thanks.

If she wanted to, she could do this forever, charge a lot of money and become rich. She has this wonderful body, with full heavy breasts and a curve to her back that makes her pliable like a toy. She wraps her legs around man number three, a long-haired artist type, and her hair shakes loose and he removes her glasses and she fucks him until he's shuddering and trying to moan, but she just keeps saying Sshhh, shhh and it's making him so happy, she keeps saying it even after he's shut up.

The morning goes by like normal except she fucks three more men, sending them out periodically to check her desk, and it's all in the silence, while people shuffle across the wood floor and trade words on paper for more words on paper.

BLISS BROYARD

My Father, Dancing

Bliss Broyard's stories have appeared in Grand Street, The Pushcart Anthology, *and* Best American Short Stories 1998. *Her debut collection,* My Father, Dancing, *was praised for its sensitivity, complexity, and wisdom. The daughter of the critic Anatole Broyard, she lives in New York City.*

As long as I can remember, my father has kept an apartment in this city where he works and I now live. In his profession, he needs to stay in touch, he has always said. That has meant spending every Monday night in the city having dinner with his associates. Occasionally, it had occurred to me that his apartment might be used for reasons other than a place to sleep after late business dinners. Then one night, while I still lived at home, my mother confided that a friend of my father's contributed one hundred dollars a month toward the rent to use it once in a while. I remember that my mother and I were eating cheese fondue for dinner. On those nights my father was away, my mother made special meals that he didn't like. She ripped off a piece of French bread from the loaf we were sharing and dipped it in the gooey mixture. "This friend brings his mistress there," she explained. "I hate that your father must be the one to supply him with a place to carry out his affair." I didn't say anything, my suspicion relieved by this sudden confidence. My mother tilted back her head and dropped the coated bread into her open mouth. When she finished chewing, she closed the subject. "His wife should know what her husband is up to. I'm going to tell her one day."

When I was walking down my father's street early last Tuesday morning, it didn't even occur to me that my father would be at his apartment. I was on my way to the subway after leaving the apartment of a man with whom I had just spent the night. This man is a friend of a man at work with whom I have also spent the night. The man at work, call him Jack, is my friend now—he said that working together made things too complicated—and we sometimes go out for a drink at the end of the day. We bumped into his friend at the bar near our office. The friend asked me to dinner and then asked me to come up to his apartment for a drink and then asked if he could make love to me. After each question, I paused before answering, suspicious because of the directness of his invitations, and then when he looked away as if it didn't really matter, I realized that, in fact, I had been waiting for these questions all night, and I would say yes.

When we walked into this man's living room, he flicked a row of switches at the entrance, turning on all the lights. He brought me a glass of wine and then excused himself to use the bathroom. I strolled over to the large picture window to admire the view. Looking out from the bright room, it was hard to make out anything on the street. The only movement was darting points of light. "It's like another world up here," I murmured under my breath. I heard the toilet flush and waited at the window. I was thinking how he could walk up behind me and drape his arm over my shoulder and say something about what he has seen out this window, and then he could take my chin and turn it toward him and we could kiss. When I didn't hear any movement behind me, I turned around. He was standing at the entrance of the room. "I'd like to make love to you," he said. "Would that be all right?" There was no music or TV, and it was so silent that I was afraid to speak. I smiled, took a sip of wine. He shifted his gaze from my face to the window behind me. I glanced out the window too, then put my glass down on the sill and nodded yes. "Why don't you take off your coat?" he said. I slipped my trench coat off my shoulders and held it in front of me. He pointed to a chair in front of the window and I draped the coat over its back. Then he asked me to take off the rest of my clothes.

Once I was naked, he just stood there staring at me. I wondered if he could see from where he was standing that I needed a bikini wax. I wanted to kiss him, we hadn't even kissed yet, and I took a small step forward and then stopped, one foot slightly in front of the other, unsteady, uncertain what to do next. "Beautiful," he finally whispered. And then he kept whispering *beautiful, beautiful, beautiful* . . .

I had just reached my father's block, though lost in my thoughts I didn't realize it, when from across the street, I heard a woman's voice. "Zachary!" the voice called out, the stress on the last syllable, the word rising in mock annoyance, the way my mother said my father's name when he teased her. All other times, she called him, as everyone else did, just Zach. I looked up and there was my father pushing a woman up against the side of a building. His building, I realized.

My father's face was buried in her neck, and she was laughing.

I recognized from her reaction that he was giving her the ticklish kind of blowing kisses that I hated. I had stopped walking and was staring at them. I caught the woman's eye briefly, and then she looked away and whispered something in my father's ear. His head jerked up and whipped around. I looked down quickly and started walking away, as if I had been caught doing something wrong. If my father had run after me and asked what I was doing in this neighborhood so early in the morning, I wouldn't have known what to tell him. I glanced back, and the woman was walking down the street the other way, and my father was standing at the entrance of his building. He was watching the woman. She was rather dressed up for so early in the morning, wearing a short black skirt, stockings, and high heels. She pulled her long blond hair out from the collar of her jacket and shook it down her back. Her gait looked slightly self-conscious, the way a woman's does when she knows she is being watched. Before I looked away, my father glanced in my direction. I avoided meeting his eyes and shook my head, a gesture I hoped he could appreciate from his distance. As I hurried to the subway, the only thought I had was fleeting: My man had not gotten up from bed to walk me out the door.

COLIN CHANNER

Waiting in Vain

Colin Channer has had his journalistic pieces published in Essence, Millimeter, Ebony Man, Black Enterprise, *and* Billboard. *His subject matter includes popular music, economics, and media technology. His short stories "The Ballad of the Sad Chanteuse" and "Black Boy, Brown Girl, Brownstones" were anthologized in* Soulfires: Young Black Men on Love and Violence. *He lives in Boston.*

SHE SAT THERE ON THE COUCH AND WATCHED HIM WATCHING HER in silence, then reached forward, held him by the chin and pulled him toward her, leaning back, opening her thighs—into whose embrace he fell, his body trembling, like hers, with need and expectation. The lights were on, and the television. They both wanted silence and darkness, but neither was willing to move, to pull away from the other's yielding flesh. They began to chafe against each other, finding crevices and surfaces to move over and under and in between, creating heat like hands being rubbed together over a feast.

Her ears, her nose, her chin, her brows—he studied them, using his tongue as a blind man would a finger, gliding over them slowly

. . . pausing . . . retracing . . . then moving forward only when he was sure that he could sketch them in detail from memory. She kissed him as he licked her, dabbing his face as if he'd been in a fight and her lips were a pair of cotton balls soaked in healing oil. She nuzzled his chin, licked his throat, and nibbled his ears before kissing him, consuming his lips hungrily, trailing her fingers through the curls at the back of his head. His tongue searched the walls of her mouth for the soaked-in memories of other men, other kisses, which he tried to cleanse away with hot saliva.

She opened his shirt, peeled it away, and began to lick his shoulders, following trails of salt to his armpits and discovering a musty sharpness like the smell of cloves. Then she took his nipples in her mouth and traced extravagant flourishes on his skin. He stood up and removed his shirt, his eyes twinkling like slices of lime in ginger beer. He had the body of a laborer. Muscular. And hard. His muscles were like crocodile backs in muddy water.

"Tell me," he said, kneeling in front of her and undoing her dress, beginning at the hem, "how do you want me to love you?"

She'd never been asked this before. Had always thought she'd want this. But now she didn't know what to say. Self-pleasure had become such a part of her because of the failings of men.

"Do anything you want," she said. "Explore me . . . teach me about myself."

She let out a gurgle when his hands touched her thighs, gliding steadily toward her hips, shoving before them a thin wave of flesh, which broke over her pelvis. He withdrew his palms to her knees then struck out again, continuing to massage her as he spoke.

"When you touch yourself," he began, "what do you imagine?"

She closed her eyes. "I'm a three-hundred-year-old mahogany

table . . . and I'm being polished, and the slightest scratch would ruin my value." She licked her fingers and stroked her belly.

"Okay," he whispered in her navel, "my tongue is a length of silk."

He began with her toes, each one, separately, then worked his way over her instep, around her ankles, over her shins and calves to her knees. He used his hands to wax her breasts as he trailed kisses up her thighs, oiled them with kisses, all the way up to the dampness where they lost a bit of their firmness and became soft, almost chewable—there, in the crevice where the smell of sweat, piss, and feminine lotions combined to make a powerful aphrodisiac. Insinuating his hands beneath her, he took the offer of her upthrust hips and rolled her panties beneath her pelvis. Waiting for him was his supper—what looked like a wet mango with a narrow gash where it had smacked the ground after falling from the tree. Nectar was pooled around the nick. He licked it.

"I like the way you taste," he said as she freed herself into nakedness. He immersed his face, smearing his cheeks, loving the wetness, inhaling the aroma, peeling away the flesh, exposing the melting pulp to his fervid breath, eating as much for his delight as hers.

As she bucked and trembled, he reached for his condoms, his tongue as fluid as a stream of water.

"Do you want to be inside me?" she asked.

He shook his head, pulled back her legs and tickled the rim of her anus, throwing a vault in her back, causing her limbs to stiffen.

"I want you inside me," she grunted. "But I want to taste you. Will you let me taste you? Fire? Please say you'll let me taste you . . ."

She kissed his torso as it passed her face, then gnawed at the hardness behind his fly, at once excited and afraid of the idea of penetration. She wanted to please him. The excitement came from this—the sweetness of surrender.

She undid his zipper with her teeth as she'd learned from movies, then leaned back a bit to appreciate the size of his wood, a sight as arresting as a *macanudo* clamped in the jaws of a child. She flicked her tongue over the tip as if it were the wheel of a lighter, then rubbed the whole length against her face, over her neck, marveling at its smoothness.

Tightening her lips like a vulva, and maneuvering her jaws to cushion her teeth, she placed a hand on his buttocks and drew him into her mouth, anticipating the fullness of having him all inside her. But he was too big. So she lavished her attention on the head, a scoop of guava sorbet—sucking it, lapping at it, using it to cool the muscles of her tired tongue.

"Let's do it now," she said as she found herself remembering Syd, as she often did while making love. "I'm worried that I might get uptight." He undressed completely and took her to bed. She opened her legs when her skin touched the sea-green sheets, and she reached for him, her palms upturned, calling him home.

SUSAN CHOI

The Foreign Student

Susan Choi was born in Indiana and grew up in Texas. Her short fiction has appeared in journals, including The Iowa Review *and* Epoch *magazine. This excerpt is from her first novel,* The Foreign Student, *which the* New Yorker *called "an auspicious debut . . . intimate in its charged description of the unlikely love affair at its core." Sue lives in New York City.*

THE INSIDE OF THE CAR WAS RUINED WITH WATER. CROOKED WINDings down the insides of the windows from where the top didn't fit had made a rising pool in each seat, marshy floorboards, every surface slippery and the windows thick with steam. They were hidden but the space was so small every contact was a struggle. They strained together, kissing hungrily until the cool tastelessness the rain had washed them with was gone, and they could taste each other's mouth. His hands touched her neck, the soft place beneath her jaw that might have never seen the sun, the cleft of her sternum where she was warm with sweat that hadn't rinsed away. He felt her inhaling the stink of his hair, pushing her tongue into his waxy, bitter ear. The storm's strength was dropping. As its noise subsided they heard their own quick breaths rising and falling, and the voices of recent bus station arrivals venturing out of the building at last and beginning to make their way across the lot toward the street. They broke apart and she found her keys. "Come on," she whispered, stamping on the gas pedal. The car started with a spluttering roar. She turned back to him triumphantly and he held her face again and kissed her even as he saw the people in the lot drawing closer, and the car's windows running with clear water, their brief shelter having dissolved.

They drove slowly along the flooded avenue, its surface chopping gently. The gutters were roaring with chocolate-colored water, tree-trash, colorful city debris. The engine gurgled as they moved, pushing a lip of water ahead of them and leaving a long V-shaped wake. They opened the windows all the way and a sultry breeze rolled across them. He smelled a rich odor of vegetable decay. When they turned onto a street lined with elevated sidewalks and storefronts, Katherine pulled to the curb. "Wait here," she said, kissing him quickly and leaping out of the car. The sun had emerged and a new day seemed to beat down on them, bright and unremitting. He looked around cautiously. The street was filling now with poststorm promenaders. A woman with a motley group of children stood talking with a man in a duster drenched black from the backs of his knees to the long hem, where it brushed his boot heels. "Our line is on the ground!" he heard her say. "A live wire laying right there in the water. Every one of these dumb kids was gonna get cooked." After she had vanished with her brood the man turned and walked up the street, splashing carelessly through the half foot of water that still ran through it. When he came level with Katherine's car he stopped and stared. Chuck's scalp prickled, and his armpits. He sat with his eyes trained ahead but feeling the man's gaze on him like a wash of unpleasant heat. Katherine came out of the store with a paper sack dangling from one hand and rushed back to the car, passing by where the man stood. Chuck felt the gaze harden further. His own heart was pounding. "Now where shall we go?" Katherine asked, smiling at him. Over her shoulder Chuck saw the man turn slowly and begin walking, frequently looking back. "Are you all right?" She touched his mouth gently. "Hungry?"

He pushed his hand into his pocket and felt the wad of money there, all his earnings in the world, plus the sharp-edged hundred-dollar bill, slightly damp. "What is a nice hotel here, where people from around the world stay?"

"The Charles," she said, without stopping to think.

They drove there, each of them for different reasons becoming more and more nervous, so that by the time they arrived they were wordlessly shy. The storm turned out to have been the outer arm of a hurricane brushing the city, and the hotel was full of well-heeled people who had just fled their estates near the coast, which were now flooded and had no electricity. They stood holding their cocktails in the lobby and swapping stories of adventure and deprivation. Chuck was given a room despite the circumstances, as he had gambled he would be. In the world of the rich, displeasure at the sight of a stranger was overruled by breeding and protocol. He paid for a week in advance, and felt a pang of excitement and terror. The desk clerk smiled a thin, artificial smile. The bellhop took his rotting, stained suitcase without the slightest flicker disturbing his inactive face, and led them to the room. When they were alone they ate the sandwiches and drank the cider she'd bought, sitting side by side on the bed in a state of near paralysis. "I can't believe it was a hurricane," Katherine said. She was talking rapidly and ceaselessly, a nervous habit he had learned to recognize. "I never see the papers anymore. I never even listen to the radio news." The afternoon was ending and the room had already grown dark. Katherine turned her watch around and around on her wrist, and he realized he had carried this gesture with him ever since the night he'd first seen her do it, when they sat together in the kitchen of Strake. "Isn't it amazing? To have come here to the city from Sewanee, and ended up even more, in a way—" He kissed her hard in the middle of her sentence and they fell backward together across the bed, their mouths making a complicated language, like a semaphore they urged against each other. They inched themselves steadily, earnestly, undeterrably up the length of the bed, their shoes and the sandwich wrappings and the cider bottles with the last sloshing inches undrunk kicked onto the floor, the difficulty of their clothing where it clung, clammy and wretched, like a no-longer-useful skin that cannot bear to be discarded, and the difficulty of the tightly made bed. They wordlessly united their efforts, pulled the bedclothes from their tuckings and wrenched them aside. He had lain facedown on his hard, slanting mattress in his North Clark Street room without moving, hardly breathing, as if an effort of his will could transport him. He'd had so little then, just the feel of her hand as it traveled his neck, or her arms around his waist as he reeled up the stairs, but those things had been singular, and total.

MARTHA COOLEY

The Archivist

Of Martha Cooley's first novel, Miranda Schwartz wrote, "The Archivist *is many things: A speculative academic mystery; a study of madness; a soliloquy to solitude." Megan Harlon called it "an engrossing, ambitious debut about love, art and insanity." It's also deeply compassionate and beautifully written. Martha Cooley lives in Brooklyn.*

JUDITH AND I WERE MARRIED IN MANHATTAN ON V-E DAY. WE were giddy with excitement, convinced that the confetti on the sidewalks had been strewn around as much for us as for the war's end. We were each twenty-seven years old and had known one another for twelve weeks. I'd escaped military service because of a lower-back condition; Judith had spent the war years in a West Side walk-up, writing poetry and working as a secretary. We'd met in a bar.

Twelve weeks. It now seems such a short stretch of time—dangerously short, really. Yet in my memory those weeks are like a honeycomb in a jar: the clustered days, suspended in an amber sweetness, drenched and happy . . .

What did I notice about her? Judith resembled no one else I

knew. My first impression was of quickness. She had a wonderfully agile, skeptical intelligence, and a certain aggressiveness—that of someone eager to engage new ideas and willing to be unsettled. Judith was less interested in Truth than in truths, and she trusted a good argument to flush them out. Right away I felt, in her company, the relief that comes when caution is unnecessary: when it is not merely possible but desirable to expose what one thinks.

She was my only genuine partner in amusement. My father had a dry, vinegary laugh; my mother's was a nervous trill, unlike the wry, detached manner of our generation. Judith was the only person who could make me laugh hard at literally nothing. She had a way of becoming suddenly, ferociously funny, and sometimes giddy and out of control, like a small child.

She loved Manhattan, and she knew it well. Among my strongest memories are our long walks, hand in hand, up and down and across the city. She liked to eat while walking—ice cream in summer, hot chestnuts in winter, apples in autumn and spring. The scent of apple on her fingertips . . .

Our long strides were evenly matched. Judith walked with purpose, deftly circumnavigating stragglers, maneuvering us through Fifth Avenue crowds, jaywalking across busy intersections. Sometimes she put her arm around my waist as we walked, and this gesture felt protective as well as affectionate, as if she were assuming responsibility for my well-being.

I doubt she knew then how much I needed to feel safe, or how deeply this need disturbed me.

Their fear of fear and frenzy, their fear of possession, of belonging to another . . . Eliot wrote of the terrors of old men, but they were mine also.

* * *

In her lovemaking Judith was candid and unpredictable. With other women I'd revealed only a self I could risk showing, polite and restrained; Judith elicited from me other selves, more demanding but also more giving. She loved me hard, without any false promising; wordlessly she urged me to learn how to please not only her but myself. Though I couldn't admit it, the force of our intimacy frightened me. I struggled to stay open, waiting for something in me to give way, to allow me to love my wife unhesitatingly.

DON DELILLO

Mao II

You want genius, I'll give you genius. Only Don DeLillo would put Frank Sinatra, Jackie Gleason, Toots Shore, and J. Edgar Hoover in the Polo Grounds—near the Giants' dugout—to watch the 1951 playoff game and see Ralph Branca throw a fast ball up and in ("not a good pitch to hit") to Bobby Thompson. He is a totally original—and quintessentially American—intellectual visionary. This excerpt is taken from his brilliant 1991 novel, Mao II.

SHE TOOK OFF HER SNEAKERS AND LAY FACEUP WITH HER CLOTHES on, suddenly wide awake. The cat appeared at her elbow, watching. She heard shouting in the street, the night voices that called all the time now, kids who pissed on sleeping men, the woman who lived in garbage bags, wearing them, sleeping inside them, who carried a large plastic bag everywhere, filled with other plastic bags. Brita heard her talking now, her voice carried on the river wind, a rasp of static in the night.

Soon the road replayed itself in her mind, the raveled passage down the hours. It was strange to lie still in a small corner and feel the power of movement, the gull-rush of air over the hood. A sense memory pulsing in the skin. The cat moved past her hand, a shrug of lunar muscle and fur. She heard car alarms going off in sequence, the panic data that fed into her life. Everything feeds in, everything is coded, there is everything and its hidden meaning. Which crisis do I trust? She felt she needed her own hidden meanings to get her through the average day. She reached out and snatched the cat, bringing it onto her chest. She thought her body had become defensive, homesick for lost assurances. It wanted to be a refuge against the way things work, against the force of what is out there. To love and touch, the roundness of these moments was crossed with something wistful now. All sex is a form of longing even as it happens. Because it happens against the crush of time. Because the surface of the act is public, a cross-grain of fear and ruin. She wanted her body to remain a secret of the past, untouched by complexity and regret. She was superstitious about talking to doctors in detail. She thought they would take her body over, name all the damaged parts, speak all the awful words. She lay for a long time with her eyes closed, trying to drift into sleep. Then she rubbed the cat's fur and felt her childhood there. It was complete in a touch, everything intact, carried out of old lost houses and fields and summer days into the river of her hand.

She slipped under the quilt, turning on her side and facing the wall to prove she was serious. Slowly now, into that helpless half-life of self-commentary, the voice film that runs between light and dark. But the time eventually came when she had to admit she was still awake. She threw off the quilt and lay there on her back. Then she climbed down the ladder and went to a window, seeing steam come heaving out of a vent hole in the street. The telephone rang. Like earthwork art, these vapor columns rising all over the city, white and silent in empty streets. She heard the machine switch on and waited for the caller to speak. A man's voice, sounding completely familiar, sounding enhanced, filling the high room, but she couldn't identify him at first, couldn't quite fix the context of his remarks, and she thought he might be someone she'd known years before, many years and very well, a voice that seemed to wrap itself around her, so strangely and totally near.

"You left without saying good-bye. Although that's not why I'm calling. I'm wide awake and need to talk to someone but that's not why I'm calling either. Do you know how strange it is for me to sit here talking to a machine? I feel like a TV set left on in an empty room. I'm playing to an empty room. This is a new kind of loneliness you're getting me into, Brita. How nice to say your name. The loneliness of knowing I won't be heard for hours or days. I imagine you're always catching up with messages. Accessing your machine from distant sites. There's a lot of violence in that phrase. 'Accessing your machine.' You need a secret code if I'm not mistaken. You enter your code in Brussels and blow up a building in Madrid. This is the dark wish that the accessing industry caters to. I'm sitting in my cane chair looking out the window. The birds are awake and so am I. Another draggy smoked-out dawn with my throat scorched raw but I've had much worse. I stopped drinking when you left last night. And I'm speaking slowly now because there's no sense of a listener, not even the silences a listener creates, a dozen different kinds, dense and expectant and bored and angry, and I feel a little awkward, making a speech to an absent friend. I hope we're friends. But that's not why I'm calling. I keep seeing my book wandering through the halls. There the thing is, creeping feebly, if you can imagine a naked humped creature with filed-down genitals, only worse, because its head bulges at the top and there's a gargoylish tongue jutting at a corner of the mouth and truly terrible feet. It tries to cling to me, to touch and fasten. A cretin, a distort. Water-bloated, slobbering, incontinent. I'm speaking slowly to get it right. It's my book after all, so I'm responsible for getting it right. The loneliness of voices stored on tape. By the time you listen to this, I'll no longer remember what I said. I'll be an old message by then, buried under many new messages. The machine makes everything a message, which narrows the range of discourse and destroys the poetry of nobody home. Home is a failed idea. People are no longer home or not home. They're either picking up or not picking up. The truth is I don't feel awkward. It's probably easier to talk to you this way. But that's not why I'm calling. I'm calling to describe the sunrise. A pale runny light spreading across the hills. There's a partial cloud cover, which makes the light seem to hug the land, quiet light, soft, calm, pale, a landglow more than a light from the sky. I thought you'd want to know these things. I thought this is a woman who wants to know these things more than other things that other people might attempt to tell her. The cloud bank is long and slate gray and altogether fine. There really isn't any more to say about it. The window is open so I can feel the air. I'm not deeply hung over and so the air does not rebuke me. The air is fine. It's precisely what it is. I'm sitting in my old cane chair with my feet up on a bench and my back to the typewriter. The birds are fine. I can hear them in the trees nearby and out in the fields, crows in clusters in the fields. The air is sharp and cold and fine and smells altogether as air should smell early on a spring morning when a man is talking to a machine. I thought these are the things this woman wants to hear about. It tries to cling to me, soft-skinned and moist, to fasten its puckery limpet flesh onto mine."

The machine cut him off.

She realized Scott was right behind her. He leaned against her, ardent and sleepy, hands reaching around, hands and thumbs, thumbs sliding into the belt loops of her jeans. She let her head drop back against his shoulder, concentrating, and he pressed in tight. She yawned and then laughed. He put his hands under her sweater, he undid her belt, leaned in to her, put his hands down along her belly, the watchfulness, the startled alert of the body to every touch. He lifted her sweater up onto her shoulders and rubbed the side of his face against her back. She concentrated, she looked like someone listening for sounds in the wall. She felt everything. She was speculative, waiting, her breathing even and careful, and she moved slowly under his hands and felt the sandy buzz of his face on her back.

She knew he would not say a word, not even going up the ladder, not even the faithful little ladder joke, and she welcomed the silence, the tactful boy lean and pale, climbing her body with a groan.

JANE DELYNN

Don Juan in the Village

Jane DeLynn is the author of the novels Some Do, In Thrall, Real Estate, *and* Don Juan in the Village, *as well as* Bad Sex Is Good, *a collection of articles and stories. To say she writes about sex is like saying Ken Griffey Jr. plays baseball. Her work is unflinchingly honest, endlessly inventive, compassionate, and intelligent.*

THE GIRL WHO HAD KNOWN BRETT WALKED OVER. "ARE YOU HAVING a good time?" she asked.

"Okay." I shrugged.

"Would you like some more coke?"

"All right."

We went into the bedroom and sat down on the bed. She spread some coke on the cover of a book she picked up. I did some lines and then some other people did too. A bunch of women were lying on the bed. If I hadn't been on coke I would never have lain down but I didn't care what people thought so I lay back on the bed with them. No one seemed to think the situation was erotic except me. They were playing Whitney Houston and James Brown. I don't usually like black music but the sound system was very good and I began to get into it. I shut my eyes. I decided this was the real, the only music, the rest was white bread and I was white bread too. For some reason I felt happy and relaxed thinking this.

In spite of the coke I began to drift off. Maybe it wasn't to sleep but just to some strange kind of place. Then I became conscious of a pleasant sensation around my neck. It felt like someone was blowing on it. When things are good there's no sense changing anything, so I didn't open my eyes. At first I thought it might be accidental, but I shifted slightly and still I felt it. There had been a curly-haired woman near where I had lain down and I was hoping this was her. I didn't want her to know I was looking so I peeked secretly through my eyelashes.

It was not the attractive, curly-haired woman but a woman whom I remembered seeing in the other room. She was fat and unattractive and I was angry at myself for having peeked, because of course I'd have to make her stop. Then I decided I didn't have to make her stop; as long as no one knew she was doing this it was all right. I mean, it was all right as long as no one knew *I* knew she was doing this. Very gently her fat fingers were brushing the hairs on the back of my neck. I told myself it was okay because we were in a room with other people and nothing would happen between her and me. But it was very exciting to be getting aroused secretly in front of the other people—even if it was by someone fat and ugly. Then I realized that her fatness and ugliness were what was making this exciting.

She began brushing the inside of my thigh. This was dangerous because it was more visible. I sneaked another look through my eyelids but people were looking out the window at some stuff. Some people were asking the woman I had come to the party with about Brett. They talked about Miami real estate for a while, then went back to New York real estate. "Maybe we should leave them alone," someone said. It took me a moment to realize they were talking about the fat woman and me. I wanted to leave with them, to show them I wasn't the type of person who would have sex with a fat person, but I realized that if they had already noticed her doing stuff to me it was too late. I decided I'd wait until they left the room, then get up and sneak out of the party and go back to the bar.

I heard the door open, the women leave. "Enjoy yourself, Shirley," one of them said. Someone laughed, then I heard the door shut. She had stopped touching me when the women left and I was about to get up when I felt her push herself off the bed and heard her move to the door. I didn't want to look like I was following her so I stayed on the bed with my eyes shut as if I really was asleep. There was a click. Could it be possible that a fat woman named Shirley had abandoned me? Then I felt rather than heard her return to the bed and plump herself down. The indentation of her weight on the futon made me roll slightly toward her. She started in on my neck again. I told myself I'd get up when she stopped. Then I felt her other hand on my pants, on top of my vagina. A searing heat kind of thing went through me that was so powerful it was all I could do not to make a noise, though I breathed a bit deeply. She unbuttoned my pants. I put my hand there as if to push hers away. "Don't worry. I locked the door," she said.

Since nobody in the party would believe I hadn't known what was going on, I decided I might as well stay. I was extremely turned on. Surely this was due to the necessity of not showing my arousal to her in any way. Nor did I open my eyes. If she knew I knew what she looked like, I'd have to leave. She unzipped my pants and stuck her hand inside my underpants. It was tight because my pants made it hard for her to maneuver her hand. "Oooh," she said when she finally got there. I was very wet. She tried to get her hand inside me but my pants were too tight. "Raise your hips," she said, "so I can take these off." She tried to pull down my pants with her other hand but I was still pretending to be half asleep, so I wouldn't move my hips. "I see," she said. She took her hand out of my underpants and put one hand under my hips and lifted me as she pulled the pants down with the other. This is an awkward thing to do, so it took a long time. Finally the pants were around my legs. Then she crawled on top of me and pushed her tongue in my mouth. She weighed a lot but I had to let her. She pushed her tongue down my throat, around my gums, and slobbered on me. It was disgusting but I was in this posture of not knowing what was happening and if I told her to stop I'd be admitting I knew. Then she pushed up my shirt and began licking around my nipple. The licking was gentle like the thing on the neck had been and I no longer wanted her to stop. She moved rhythmically in a circle, and my body did too. I thought I heard her say, "Aha!" but I wasn't sure. As she continued to do this she shifted her weight so most of it was on my right side, then she put her hand back between my legs. "Oooh," she said. She took some goo and rubbed it on my thigh, then she lifted her tongue from my nipple and put the hand with my goo on it on my face. It felt like the sticky part of an egg. Her elbow dug into me as she supported herself. Then she lowered herself down my body. It felt heavy but somehow comfortable. She put her mouth around my nipple again but this time after a few gentle licks she began to bite. It hurt, but of course I couldn't say "ow." I tried to squirm but she held me down so I couldn't get away. Just when it was about to become too much she went back to the licks for a bit, and so on. She moved her hand back to my vagina. She flicked it a few times then put a finger inside me. "Spread your legs," she said. Although I wanted to I didn't. She moved my legs as far apart as she could with the pants still around my ankles, then she must have decided this wasn't enough, for she got off the bed, ripped off my shoes without even untying the laces, and pulled off my pants. She shoved my legs apart with both hands. She sat down between them and began pulling at the hairs around my vagina. She bit the inside of my thighs a few times, then put a finger in me. I moved to get it in deeper. Then she stuck two more fingers inside me. At first this felt good, but she spread me even farther apart and pushed even more deeply into me. It hurt a little, but in the right kind of way. Her hand was on my right leg as she balanced herself. She shoved her hand in and out as if we were fucking. It made an embarrassing sucking noise. I could hear it clearly because there was no more music in the room, though I could hear it in the party outside.

Then I felt a real pain. I couldn't tell exactly what was happening. First I thought she was trying to put her thumb inside me, then I decided she was curling her fingers into a fist. I felt like I could be split apart, but I told myself that babies' heads came out of there, it must be large enough. I heard myself making noise—"uh . . . uh . . ."—a kind of grunt. The upper part of my body rocked a bit, but she crawled on top of me to hold me down. I wanted to tell her she was really hurting me but the longer this went on the harder it was to talk. I told myself to relax, to let her hand in. She began sucking on my ear, then she dribbled into it.

She licked my neck and I felt like a cat, arching it, then she began to suck. This was terrible because it would make a hickey but it seemed stupid to tell her to stop this when she was doing something much worse to my vagina. She began sucking right around the center of my throat and it was very ticklish but pleasant and when I stopped moving my neck I realized that her entire fist was inside me and my body had closed itself around her hand. I told myself to be careful how I moved so she wouldn't rip me apart. There was pain there but so much so it had become a kind of numbness so that I almost couldn't feel anything, and yet it was extremely satisfying, maybe because for once there was no place left to go. She knew all my secrets, at least all the secrets in this part of my body, which at the time seemed the only important thing. She spread her fist open a bit and I tried to breathe into the pain so we could be in it together. She moved her hand, and I breathed, then I felt a part of my body that had never been touched be touched. Through the walls of my vagina she was touching other organs. It was frightening but fascinating. It was like a tickle deep inside that you wanted to be scratched. But if she scratched she could break through and I could get peritonitis and die. It occurred to me how odd it would be if I got peritonitis from this fat woman whose last name I didn't even know, and died. What if there was dirt in her fingernails and they scraped my vagina? I felt I could scream from the tickling. As if she were reading my mind she spread the fist so the pain increased to balance the tickling and I could stand it. They canceled each other out. Janis Joplin was singing ". . . take another little piece of my heart, baby" in the other room—a very clear version that I decided had to be a CD. It reminded me once again about dying. I had never heard of a woman dying from this and I decided I was just having an anxiety attack, like I did when I thought I couldn't breathe. I used to have them all the time when I had sex but I had kept breathing, hadn't I? But of course this woman might have lost all her judgment from coke. I didn't know if she had been doing coke or not. For all I knew she could have done some of that new blotter acid that was said to be going around and could be really nuts. For all I knew, Brett's friend had slipped blotter acid into my drink and *I* was the one who was nuts. For all I knew the whole thing had been planned as a setup for the fat woman.

"Try to relax," she said. "I'm coming out."

This hurt much more than her entering, because I wasn't so excited. I bit my lip to compensate for the pain—the way her spreading her fist inside had compensated for the tickle—so I wouldn't say "ow."

The fist was out. I felt exhausted and depressed. Her breath smelled bad as she kissed me. The whole thing seemed stupid and dangerous and far away.

She was off me. I suddenly realized how hard it had been to breathe. The gunk on my body began to evaporate and I felt cold. The bed rose a little as she stood up. I heard her moving around. I assumed she was straightening herself up. As soon as she left I would get dressed and leave the party. The only person who knew me here was Brett's friend; if I were lucky she had already gone home.

"Open your eyes." If I hadn't while her fist was forcing its way into my body, I sure wasn't going to now. "Come on, open your eyes." I could feel the bed sinking under her weight again. "Or I'll take your pants into the other room."

I opened my eyes. Now that I was no longer excited, she seemed even worse than when I had glimpsed her through my eyelashes. She leaned forward to kiss me but I turned aside my head.

Her hand was on my nipple. I tried to push it away but she pinched it tightly. "Ow," I said, since my eyes were open.

"Ow, my ass! You little slut," she said. We stared at each other, registering the disgust in each other's eyes. Without another word she left the room.

I sat up, pulled on my pants, and bent down to look for my shoes. As I straightened up I heard a click, then the smell of gas, then the sound and smell of paper being burned.

I turned around. Brett's friend was sitting there, in a chair, puffing contentedly on a cigarette.

"Have a good time?" she asked.

E. L. DOCTOROW

Billy Bathgate

With the accumulation of E. L. Doctorow's innumerable honors, it becomes increasingly (and embarrassingly) obvious that he deserves the Nobel Prize. This excerpt shows him at the height of his powers in what is undoubtedly the best sex-plus-nature scene in all of American literature.

THE THING ABOUT DREW WAS SHE WAS NOT GENITALLY DIRECT, SHE wanted to kiss my ribs and my white boyish chest, she held my legs and ran her hands up and down the backs of my thighs, she caressed my ass and sucked my earlobes and my mouth, and she did all these things as if they were all that she wanted, she made small editorial sounds of approval or delectation, as a commentator to the action, little single high notes, whispers without words like remarks to herself, it was as if she was consuming me as an act of eating and drinking, and it wasn't designed to arouse me, what boy in that situation needed arousal? from the moment she stopped the car I was tumescent, and I waited for some acknowledgment from her that this was in fact part of me too but it didn't come and it didn't come and I flared through my need into an exquisite pain, I thought I would go mad, I became agitated and discovered only then her availability, that in all of this she was only waiting for me to find her absolute willingness to be still and listen to me for a change. This was so girlish of her, so surprisingly restrained and submissive, I was not artful but simply myself and this brought forth from her a conspiratorial laughter, it gave her the pleasure of generosity to have me in her, it was not an excitement but more like a happiness of having this boy in her, she wrapped her legs around my back and I rocked us up and down in the backseat of the car with my feet sticking out of the open door, and when I came she held her arms around me tight enough to stop my breath and she sobbed and kissed my face as if something terrible had happened to me, as if I had been wounded and she was, in an act of desperate compassion, trying to make it as if it had not happened.

Then I was following her stark naked through the brush into this noplace of such great green presence she had chosen arbitrarily or by happenstance, with her gift for centering the world around herself, so that it was all very beautifully central in my mind, the place to be, following her flashing white form around trees, under tangles, avoiding the whip of branches, with a brilliant chatter of communities of unseen birds telling me how late I was to have found it. And then we were going generally downward, and the ground became swampy and the air close and I found myself slapping at stings in my skin, I had wanted to catch her, tackle her and fuck her again, and she was doing this to me, taking me into furies of mosquitoes. But I came upon her squatting and ladling handfuls of mud over herself and we applied this cold mud to each other and then we walked like children into the sinking darkness of forest, hand in hand like fairy-tale children in deep and terrible trouble, as indeed we were, and then we found ourselves at this still pond as black as I had ever seen water to be and of course she waded in and bid me to follow and my God it was fetid, it was warm and scummy, my feet were in wet mats of pond weed, I treaded water to keep my feet from sinking and couldn't crawl back out fast enough, but she swam on her back a few yards and then came crawling out on all fours, and she was covered with this invisible slime, her body was slimed as mine was and we lay in this mud and I punched into her and held her blond head back in the mud and pumped slime up her and we lay there rutting in this foul fen and I came and held her down and wouldn't let her move, but lay in her with her breath loud in my ear, and when I lifted my head and looked into her alarmed green eyes in their panic of loss, I grew hard again right in her and she began to move, and this time we had the time, by the third time it takes its time, and I found the primeval voice in her, like a death rattle, a shrill sexless bark, over and over again as I jammed into her, and it became tremulous a terrible crying despair, and then she screamed so shriekingly I thought something was wrong and reared to look at her, her lips were pulled back over her teeth and her green eyes dimmed as I looked in them, they had lost sight, gone flat, as if her mind had collapsed, as if time had turned in her and she had passed back into infancy and reverted through birth into nothingness, and for an instant they were no longer eyes, for an instant they were about to be eyes, the eyes of soullessness.

Yet a few moments later she was smiling and kissing me and hugging me as if I had done something dear, brought her a flower or something.

* * *

When we staggered upright globs of mud fell from us, she laughed and turned to show me the back of her, absent in darkness, as if she had been cleaved in half, with the front of her shiny and swollen into sculpture. Even her golden head seemed halved. There was nothing for it but to go back into the pond, and then she swam further out and insisted I come after her, and the water grew cooler, it was deeper and it went on behind a bend, I swam with her stroke for stroke, giving her my best YMCA crawl, and we came out on the bank on the far side, washed clean of mud and somewhat less slick.

By the time we got back to the car we were dry, but putting clothes on was uncomfortable, as if we were covering extreme sunburns, we smelled of pond scum, we smelled like frogs, we drove off trying not to lean back in the seats and several miles down the road we came to this motor court and rented a cabin and we stood together in the shower and washed each other with a big cake of white soap and stood holding each other under the water, and then we lay on the top of the bed and she curled herself along my side with my arm around her, and perhaps created with that nuzzling gesture the moment of our truest intimacy, when by some shuddering retrenchment of her being she matched me in age and yearning for sophistication, like a boy's girlfriend, only two bodies between us and a long life ahead of terrible surprises. So I felt a kind of fearful pride. I knew I could never have the woman Mr. Schultz had had, just as he hadn't known the woman Bo Weinberg had known, because she covered her tracks, she trailed no history, suiting herself to the moment, getting her gangsters or her boys in transformative stunts of the spirit, she would never write her memoirs, this one, not even if she ever lived to an old age, she would never tell her life because she needed no one's admiration or sympathy or wonder, and because all judgments, including love, came of a language of complacency she had never wasted her time to master. So it all worked out, how protective I felt there in that cabin, I let her doze on my arm and studied a fly drifting into its caroming angles under the roof and understood that Drew Preston granted absolution, it was what you got instead of a future with her. Clearly she would not be interested in the enterprise of keeping us alive, so I would have to do that for both of us.

SUSAN M. DODD

Hell-Bent Men and Their Cities

Susan M. Dodd has taught at Bennington, Harvard, and the Iowa Writers' Workshop. She is the author of several critically acclaimed books, including Mamaw, Old Wives' Tales, No Earthly Notion, The Mourner's Bench, *and* Hell-Bent Men and Their Cities. *She lives in Ocracoke, North Carolina.*

INEVITABLY, THEY MADE LOVE. HER RESERVATIONS WERE DELICATE, ladylike. His eagerness suggested chivalry. The city disappeared. The country grew remote and foreign. They made love beautifully.

She cried a little bit, barely making a sound.

"Why would you want to cry?" he asked her.

She did not tell him, but she knew: a sense of loss attended her passion, because she had thought it driven out long ago. And vanished passion had been her only victory for many years.

He leaned over her, shielding her face, a gesture of infinite tact. Almost as if he shared her loss.

He had bought new bedsheets for her visit from the country. Edged with embroidered buterflies, they were nothing he'd have chosen for himself. He wanted her, he said, to feel at home in the city. As she lay beside him, tangled in the stiff new percale, she suffered premonitions of a regret she couldn't feel now. She knew that the moment she got home, she would transform his desire into courtesy, her own into miscalculation.

Late-afternoon sun slanted through his sooty window. Below blinds at half-mast not a tree was in sight. Outside on the avenue rush hour was starting. Whistles and sirens, clanging and shouts. Ominous rumbles trapped underground. She tried to imagine preparations for a circus or parade, a public spectacle to welcome her to the city. But the throng she conjured up brought to mind only abandonment, abuse. She wanted to go home . . .

If only he would come with her. His well-being suddenly seemed as vital and tenuous as her own. She wanted to spare him, to lure him to a safe, still place.

He pulled her closer. "Was it—?"

She could not, at this moment, abide hearing him say something ordinary. She pressed her finger to his lips and shook her head.

His lips parted.

She shut her eyes.

He pulled her fingertip into his mouth like the last morsel of an exquisite meal. He was extraordinary.

Did he still mean to show her a museum? she wondered. Discuss business?

"There's something you want to ask me," he said.

She leaned forward so that her hair descended between them like a scrim.

"How?" she whispered.

She was never sure if he heard her. It was an indelicate question, anyway.

They made love again. Her expensive suit lay in a heap on the floor. Her silk blouse, fragile as ash, hovered on the footboard of his bed. She saw that he had fallen asleep, his face so shockingly innocent that he seemed to resemble her.

Very carefully, she slipped from the bed to kneel on the floor, where their shoes lay scattered together. She studied their random pattern for a long time. Then she set them side by side, in a straight row, his worn oxfords bracketing her sharp untried heels.

RIKKI DUCORNET

The Word "Desire"

Rikki Ducornet's fictional works include The Stain, Entering Fire, The Fountains of Neptune, The Jade Cabinet, Phosphor in Dreamland, *and most recently,* The Fan-Maker's Inquisition. *She has also published six volumes of poetry, two children's books, and has exhibited her drawings and prints throughout the world. She is a writer's writer. Her works are totally unique in both form and content. Rikki Ducornet's world is a place of enchanted beauty, linguistic sensuality and lush carnality.*

SHE AWAKENS LATE, THEIR LIMBS IN DISORDER, HIS HEART QUICK against her ribs. She feels his cock stir against her thigh. She imagines it has a life of its own because although he appears to be fast asleep, his cock is wide awake, *its own animal* she thinks, thick and hard and thrashing. He sighs, opens his eyes, laughs softly, and with his body covers her. Taking her wrists in his hands he enters her.

She is still wet from the last time—when was it? *Once, twice,* in the middle of the night. They are new lovers—or so it seems; they have been lovers for two years now, perhaps longer. It has always been impossible for her to keep track of the time, to recall when things have taken place, even important things. She cannot remember when it was that he took her for the first time, but will never forget that wealth of dark delight. *Unlike anything else.* He is saying it now: *unlike anything ever known before.* A lucent event like a trespass within a sacred space. When he fucks her, as he is fucking her now, she loses specificity; she crosses over the threshold from solid to fluid, steps into a tender vortex, into a moon-drenched sea, a sun-drenched country.

NOW THEY ARE ON THE HIGHWAY HEADING WEST. THE LANDSCAPE opens before them like a body: it spreads and heaves. And they, they are at the heart of the world; they are in its hand and at the center of its eye. They *are* the eye of the world: at their retina's surface the desert burns. She is luxuriating, gazing out, thinking how the word "desire" illuminates their lives; how far the word "desire" has taken them. From time to time she moves her face against his arm, or takes his hand to her lips to gently bite his fingers, suck his fingers, causing him to laugh, to reach over and put his hand between her legs, to, with intimacy, explore her. For a moment the sun ignites the car. She thinks how before electricity the sun was a great power, was *the* great power. She thinks how the world oscillates about this power. An interminable event of seduction. She thinks: *Gravity is a species of fascination.*

NOW THEY SEE THE RUINS RISING ALONG THE RIM OF THE SKY, espousing the cliffs—a natural fortress—all openings facing outward. They have left behind rubble and scree, low-growing sage, scrub oak, and are entering a woodland. For a few moments the ruins and the cliff are concealed. Just before they pull into the parking lot, a jeweled lizard runs across the road on its hind legs, runs with the vibrancy and purpose of a sacred thing, before vanishing.

They begin their climb. The paths are narrow, cut into stone. The ancient city rises above them like many faces, numberless eyes and mouths open for speaking. The city is as simple as the bones of an animal and it is painful to imagine the landscape without it: it is like imagining an animal without its spine. They continue to climb, and soon the city dissolves beneath them. They have reached a sacred place, a bowl-shaped platform seemingly suspended in the air and reflecting the sun like a mirror of polished metal. As the sun spills down the flanks of the mountain opposite, dazzling her where she stands, she is seized by the primacy of the moment and she imagines all those who have stood as she stands, illumed and warmed by the sun. She imagines all those who will come after, virtual strangers like blossoms threaded by time into garlands. Wanting to say: *I feel so alive!* She turns to him.

But he is not looking to the mountains; he does not see the sun spilling into the valley. Instead he is gazing with intensity toward the path. There is heat in his eyes, a fire she knows well: it is the fire of their first encounter, a look of dark avowal; his gaze is directed like an arrow of fire across the way to a woman who is standing alone gazing—as she has been gazing—to the west. The woman is beautiful—his *type* she thinks, *dark, like me*. The woman stands still, so still beneath his gaze in that sacred theater, that it is clear to her the woman knows she is being watched. *Who is the trespasser here? How can this be?* How can this be that he stands on his own piece of turf as it were, stands apart from her, out of her orbit, so distant as though nothing joined them? Had ever joined them? Not a thread of saliva, nor an amorous word.

Now the air is very thin. Her bones, too, are thin, and her skin (above all her skin!) so thin it no longer keeps her warm. For a moment she longs to dissolve, to vanish, to vanish into the other woman. To be the other woman; to lift her eyes and take in his gaze for the first time. To receive his gaze as a landscape is flooded with sunlight.

A curious inversion takes hold. As she looks at him gazing at the other woman, she is no longer looking at him, but looking from within him. She has become his eyes, so to speak. The immeasurable distance she had imagined between them has vanished. And this bewitching inversion does not stop there because suddenly she *is* the other woman, aware that he is gazing at her. He, a stranger now, is seizing her with his eyes, entering her with his gaze, possessing her. His eyes are like daggers of light, as though fucking were an attribute of light, as though looking were consuming, and the retina a place of burning.

Because she is an artist, she knows the eye hungers. At that moment it is revealed to her that her lover is seeing with his sexual soul, that his eyes are revealing this most compassionate place within himself. She knows this place intimately and yet as often as she has entered there, has been irresistibly drawn there, still it remains a power and a mystery. Gazing through his eyes at the other, receiving her lover's heat through the other's body, it is revealed to her that she is not dreaming nor inventing this, but that she is witness to a simple and essential experience of seeing. And being.

An instant later, vertigo overtakes her. She thinks: *But what will happen?* And she catches her breath. He turns to her then and says:

Shall we go? She cannot meet his eyes now—her own eyes are so thin with seeing they are a fragile paper. Should he look into them, they will tear. As though glued to the spot, looking into the sun, she nods. He says: *It is beautiful.* She wonders: *What is he naming beautiful? And who?*

The other has turned away; she has begun to move gracefully—an agile female animal—down the path. She admires the woman's animal movements. Something about the way she moves reveals that she knows he is still watching her and *it is true,* she thinks, *her form is lovely, her gaze bewitching; has he tired of me so quickly? What will happen? And what is this power that opens and shuts within me like the eye of a camera? And who are the trespassers here? And who are the seekers?* She knows the answer: They are all seekers. She thinks: *How far the word "desire" goes! How it tugs us along! How it worries us, daggers us! How it lights our path.*

They descend into trees and the path becomes many paths. Theirs heads east and now they are alone. Like a light gone out, like an extinguished flame, the other woman is gone without a trace. She feels this. In her bones and blood she feels this: the other has left no trace. She feels his heat, his substantiality, his intelligence receiving the world. Even before he reaches out to put his hand gently at the back of her neck she quickens; her skin fits over her muscles and bones exactly.

EVER AFTER, EACH TIME HE EMBRACES HER, THE OTHER WOMAN and her vanishment informs her passion—not because the fear of his loss excites her lust, but because the other woman revealed this: Desire is a figment swiftly fleeting, an ephemeral enactment upon the finite stage of the mutable world, and flesh a flame and a seeming *Is it true then,* she thinks, *all is fire?* This knowledge, given her by her rival, her sister, the stranger, fans the pleasure she shares with him, instants of delight dissolving as they happen, collapsing into themselves just as time collapses into itself, and as the two of them collapse into one another after love.

You see: it was as if that afternoon she had stepped over a threshold. Thereafter she thinks: *He and I share the same mystery*. Except she believes this: she believes that she is the one who keeps this particular mystery hidden. She believes that he has forgotten the other woman, that the other woman has been replaced over and over again by other chance encounters, other faces igniting the world like suns. And she believes that each time he embraces her, her own body eclipses the others, or—better still—*exemplifies* the others. So that her intimate life with him is a fusion of memory and desire and will: the will to be unique, to be uniquely his, to live each unique instant fully—and the will to *be* desire, to be the infinite faces of desire; to be one word and that word is "desire."

Now she has, at least to herself, confessed everything. There is nothing more to confess, except this, and to him: that when she takes his sex into her mouth, between her teeth, against her tongue; when his sex sweetly collides with the back of her throat like a comet hitting the world; when as he enters her face he holds her head between his hands or caresses her hair, her body dissolves into time and she has become an event of lucency. She has become heat and light dissolving between his fingers, the seconds like hot sand spilling through his fingers . . . and then his sperm like a nectar burning in her throat.

DAVID EBERSHOFF

The Danish Girl

David Ebershoff is the publishing director of the Modern Library, a division of Random House. His first novel, The Danish Girl, *based on the life of the painter Einar Wegener, who, in 1931, became the first man ever to be transformed surgically into a woman, is an imaginative, intelligent, and moving love story.*

THEY RENTED AN APARTMENT IN A CUT-STONE TOWNHOUSE ON THE rue Vieille du Temple. The apartment was on the fourth floor, the top, with skylights cut into the steep roof and windows facing the street. The rear faced the courtyard, where during the summer geraniums grew in window boxes wired to the ledges and laundry stiffened on the line. The townhouse was just down the street from the Hôtel de Rohan, with its entrance curving into the sidewalk and the two great black doors of its gate. The street was narrow but drained well in winter, and sliced through the Marais with its grand hôtels reconfigured as government offices or warehouses for dry-goods importers or simply abandoned, and its Jewish shops, where Einar and Greta would buy dried fruit and sandwiches on Sundays when everything else was closed.

The apartment had two workrooms. Einar's, with a few landscapes of the bog perched on oversized easels. And Greta's, with her Lili paintings, sold before they dried, and the spot on the wall, perpetually wet and thick, where she dabbed out her colors until they were just right: the brown of Lili's hair, which turned to honey after one swim in an August sea; the purply red of the blush that clasped around the base of her throat; the silvery white of the inside of her elbows. Each workroom had a daybed covered with kilims. Sometimes at night Greta would sleep there when she was too tired to climb into the bed they shared in the little room at the back of the apartment, where there was a darkness that felt to Einar like a cocoon. In their bedroom, with the lamps turned off, it was too dark for Einar to see even his hand in front of his face, and this he liked, and he'd lie there until dawn, when the laundry pulley would squeak and one of their neighbors would get busy hanging out another load.

In the summer mornings Lili would rise and ride the omnibus down to the Bains du pont-Solférino on the quai des Tuileries. The pool had a row of changing cabanas that were made of striped canvas, like tall, narrow tents. Inside Lili would change into her bathing dress, carefully arranging herself beneath the frilled skirt so that she could remain, as she thought of it, modest. Since they left Denmark her body had changed, and now her breasts were fleshy with muscle gone soft, enough to fill the little dented cups of her bathing dress. Her rubber bathing cap, with its pneumatic smell, would pull her hair back, tugging on her cheeks and giving her an exotic look with her eyes slanted and her mouth flattened out. Lili had learned to carry a hand mirror with her, and in the canvas cabana, in the summer mornings, she would look at herself, waving the mirror across each inch of her skin, until the pool attendant would flap the canvas and demand if mademoiselle needed some assistance.

With that, Lili would slip into the pool, holding her head above the water. She would bathe for thirty minutes, her shoulders turning as each arm lifted over her head with the motion of a windmill, until the other women in the pool—for this pool, like the tearoom where she sometimes took her coffee and croissant, was reserved for ladies—would stop and hang on to the lip of the pool to watch little Lili, so graceful, so long-armed, so, they would cluck, *puissante*.

It was what she liked most: her head gliding across the surface of the pool like a little duck; the other ladies in their wool bathing dresses watching her with their mixture of indifference and gossipy intrigue; the way she could pull herself from the pool, her fingertips pruned, and pat the towel down her arms as she dried in the glittering light that reflected off the Seine. She would watch the traffic across the river. And Lili would think that all of this was possible because she and Greta had left Denmark. She would think, in the summer mornings, on the lip of the pool filled with Seine water, that she was free. Paris had freed her. Greta had freed her. Einar, she would think, was slipping away. Einar was freeing her. A shiver would run up her damp spine; her shoulders would shudder.

In the cabana, after returning the pink towel to the attendant, she would peel off the bathing dress, and if she was in a particularly strong trance about her life and the possibility of it all, she would let out a little gasp when she discovered that down there, between her white, goose-pimpled thighs, lay a certain shriveled thing. It was so vile to her that she would snap closed her thighs, tucking it away, her knee bones smacking; she could hear the muffled smack, and the sound of it—like two felt-wrapped cymbals meeting in crescendo—would remind Lili, would remind Einar, of the girl at Madame Jasmin-Carton's who had danced resentfully and snapped her knees together in such a harsh manner that he could hear the smack of bone even through the smudged glass.

And so there Einar would be—a little Danish man in the changing cabana of Paris's finest ladies' pool. At first he would be confused, his face blank in the hand mirror. He wouldn't know where he was, couldn't recognize the reverse stripes of the inside of the cabana's canvas. Didn't recognize the slip and splash of the ladies swimming laps. The only clothing on the hanger was a simple brown dress with a belt. Black shoes with wedgy heels. A purse with a few coins and a lipstick. A chiffon scarf patterned with pears. He was a man, he would suddenly think, and yet he had no way back to the apartment unless he put on all these clothes. Then he'd see the double string of Danish amber beads; his grandmother had worn them her whole life, even when farming the sphagnum fields, the beads around her throat clickety-clacketing against her sternum as she stooped to fill in the hole of a red fox. She had given them to Greta, who hated amber, who gave them to Einar; and Einar—he recalled—gave them to a little girl named Lili.

It came to him like that: in pieces, slowly, triggered by the amber beads or the swat of the attendant's hand against the canvas door as she inquired once again whether mademoiselle needed assistance. He would put on the brown dress and the wedgy shoes as best he could. He would burn with shame as he clasped the belt, although now it would seem to him that he knew nothing about the tricky snaps and clasps of a woman's dress. His purse held only a few francs; more weren't coming for another three days, he knew.

But Einar would decide against walking and take a cab back to the apartment because the discomfort of the brown dress was too much to bear on the streets of Paris. The scarf hung over the back of the chair, nearly fluttering on its own, and Einar couldn't bear to tie it over his head and around his throat. It looked as if it might strangle him, the gauzy chiffon with the yellow pears. It belonged to someone else.

And so Einar would set out from the ladies' pool in Lili's clothes, with the rubber bathing cap still on his head, dropping a franc into the attendant's ever-extended hand, gliding like the little duck on the pool's surface, above the whispery gossip of the French ladies who would linger at the pool until it was time to return home and help their Polish maids prepare lunch for their pinafored children, while Einar, sloppy and red-eyed in Lili's clothes, would return to Greta, who, in the course of the morning, had set the props and sketched the study for another painting of Lili.

NATHAN ENGLANDER

For the Relief of Unbearable Urges

Nathan Englander grew up in New York. He is a graduate of the Iowa Writers' Workshop and a recent recipient of the Pushcart Prize. His stories have appeared in Story Magazine *and* The New Yorker. *His debut collection,* For the Relief of Unbearable Urges, *was a major literary event and rightly so. It's not everybody who can elicit both laughter and tears—plus invoke the ghosts of Isaac Bashevis Singer and John Cheever—in the same story. He lives in Jerusalem.*

THE FIRST TIME PAST, HE DID NOT STOP, DRIVING BY THE WOMEN at high speed and taking the curves around the cement island so that his wheels screeched and he could smell the burning rubber. Dov Binyamin slowed down, trying to maintain control of himself and the car, afraid that he had already drawn too much attention his way. The steering wheel began to vibrate in Dov's shaking hands. The Rebbe had given him permission, had instructed him. Was not the Rebbe's heter valid? This is what Dov Binyamin told his hands, but they continued to tremble in protest.

On his second time past, a woman approached the passenger door. She wore a matching shirt and pants. The outfit clung tightly, and Dov could see the full form of her body. Such immodesty! She tapped at the window. Dov Binyamin reached over to roll it down. Flustered, he knocked the gear-shift, and the car lurched forward. Applying the parking brake, he opened the window the rest of the way.

"Close your lights," she instructed him. "We don't need to be onstage out here."

"Sorry," he said, shutting off the lights. He was comforted by the error, not wanting the woman to think he was the kind of man who employed prostitutes on a regular basis.

"You interested in some action?"

"Me?"

"A shy one," she said. She leaned through the window, and Dov Binyamin looked away from her large breasts. "Is this your first time? Don't worry. I'll be gentle. I know how to treat a black hat."

Dov Binyamin felt the full weight of what he was doing. He was giving a bad name to all Hasidim. It was a sin against God's name. The urge to drive off, to race back to Jerusalem and the silence of his wife, came over Dov Binyamin. He concentrated on his dispensation.

"What would you know from black hats?" he said.

"Plenty," she said. And then, leaning in farther, "Actually, you look familiar." Dov Binyamin seized up, only to begin shaking twice as hard. He shifted into first and gave the car some gas. The prostitute barely got clear of the window.

When it seemed as if he wouldn't find a suitable match, a strong-looking young woman stepped out of the darkness.

"Good evening," he said.

She did not answer or ask any questions or smile. She opened the passenger door and sat down.

"What do you think you're doing?"

"Saving you the trouble of driving around until the sun comes up." She was American. He could hear it. But she spoke beautiful Hebrew, sweet and strong as her step. Dov Binyamin turned on his headlights and again bumped the gearshift so that the car jumped.

"Settle down there, Tiger," she said. "The hard part's over. All the rest of the work is mine."

THE ROOM WAS IN AN UNLICENSED HOSTEL. IT HAD ITS OWN ENtrance. There was no furniture other than a double bed and three singles. The only lamp stood next to the door.

The prostitute sat on the big bed with her legs curled underneath her. She said her name was Devorah.

"Like the prophetess," Dov Binyamin said.

"Exactly," Devorah said. "But I can only see into the immediate future."

"Still, it is a rare gift with which to have been endowed." Dov shifted his weight from foot to foot. He stood next to the large bed unable to bring himself to bend his knees.

"Not really," she said. "All my clients already know what's in store."

She was fiery, this one. And their conversation served to warm up the parts of Dov the heat wave had not touched. The desire that had been building in Dov over the many months so filled his body that he was surprised his skin did not burst from the pressure.

He tossed his hat onto the opposite single, hoping to appear at ease, as sure of himself as the hairy-chested cabdriver with his cigarettes. The hat landed brim side down. Dov's muscles twitched reflexively, though he did not flip it onto its crown.

"Wouldn't you rather make your living as a prophetess?" he asked.

"Of course. Prophesying's a piece of cake. You don't have to primp all day for it. And it's much easier on the back, no wear and tear. Better for *you*, too. At least you'd leave with something in the morning." She took out one of her earrings, then, as an afterthought, put it back in. "Doesn't matter anyway. No money in it. They pay me to do everything *except* look into the future."

"I'll be the first then," he said, starting to feel almost comfortable. "Tell me what you see."

She closed her eyes and tilted her head so that her lips began to part, this in the style of those who peer into other realms. "I predict that this is the first time you've done such a thing."

"That is not a prophecy. It's a guess." Dov Binyamin cleared his throat and wiggled his toes against the tops of his shoes. "What else do you predict?"

She massaged her temples and held back a naughty grin.

"That you will, for once, get properly laid."

But this was too much for Dov Binyamin. Boiling in the heat and his shame, he motioned toward his hat.

Devorah took his hand.

"Forgive me," she said, "I didn't mean to be crude."

Her fingers were tan and thin, more delicate than Chava's. How strange it was to see strange fingers against the whiteness of his own.

"Excluding the affections of my mother, blessed be her memory, this is the first time I have been touched by a woman that is not my wife."

She released her grasp and, before he had time to step away, reached out for him again, this time more firmly, as if shaking on a deal. Devorah raised herself up and straightened a leg, displayed it for a moment, and then let it dangle over the side of the bed. Dov admired the leg, and the fingers resting against his palm.

"Why are we here together?" she asked—she was not mocking him. Devorah pulled at the hand and he sat at her side.

"To relieve my unbearable urges. So that my wife will be able to love me again."

Devorah raised her eyebrows and pursed her lips.

"You come to me for your wife's sake?"

"Yes."

"You are a very dedicated husband."

She gave him a smile that said, You won't go through with it. The smile lingered, and then he saw that it said something completely different, something irresistible. And he wondered, as a shiver ran from the trunk of his body out to the hand she held, if what they say about American women is true.

Dov walked toward the door, not to leave, but to shut off the lamp.

"One minute," Devorah said, reaching back and removing a condom from a tiny pocket—no more than a slit in the smooth black fabric of her pants. Dov Binyamin knew what it was and waved it away.

"Am I really your second?" she asked.

Dov heard more in the question than was intended. He heard

a flirtation; he heard a woman who treated the act of being second as if it were special. He was sad for her—wondering if she had ever been anyone's first. He did not answer out loud, but instead nodded, affirming.

Devorah pouted as she decided, the prophylactic held between two fingers like a quarter poised at the mouth of a jukebox. Dov switched off the light and took a half step toward the bed. He stroked at the darkness, moving forward until he found her hair, soft, alive, without any of the worked-over stiffness of Chava's wigs.

"My God," he said, snatching back his hand as if he had been stung. It was too late, though. That he already knew. The hunger had flooded his whole self. His heart was swollen with it, pumping so loudly and with such strength that it overpowered whatever sense he might have had. For whom then, he wondered, was he putting on, in darkness, such a bashful show? He reached out again and stroked her hair, shaking but sure of his intent. With his other arm, the weaker arm, to which he bound every morning his tefillin, the arm closer to the violent force of his heart, he searched for her hand.

Dov found it and took hold of it, first roughly, as if desperate. Then he held it lightly, delicately, as if it were made of blown glass—a goblet from which, with ceremony, he wished to drink. Bringing it toward his mouth, he began to speak.

"It is a sin to spill seed in vain," he said, and Devorah let the condom fall at the sound of his words.

TIM FARRINGTON

Blues for Hannah

In the age of constant sound-bite hype, Tim Farrington's Blues for Hannah *is a welcome respite. It is a novel of quiet intelligence and graceful poignancy, as is his previous novel,* California Book of the Dead. *He lives in San Francisco with his wife, Claire.*

HANNAH AND I LEFT LATE IN THE DAY, A WEEK BEFORE HALLOWEEN, in the face of warnings of an early storm that Hannah said we could beat to the mountains. We ran ahead of the weather front most of the way, passing through South Lake Tahoe on dry streets at around midnight and turning south on 395 as the first snowflakes began to fall. Most of the little roadside motels were closed up for the night by then, and we drove another two hours south before we found a place that would take us in. The sleepy guy at the desk gave us a room with a queen-size bed. Rather than wake him up again to ask for singles, Hannah and I climbed chastely in from opposite sides, relying on our spiritual maturity and well-established friendship to keep us warm and separate through the night.

For one long moment, it even seemed possible. Hannah said good night and rolled over with her back to me, quite properly. We lay quietly in the darkness with the sheet still cool between us.

But I was aware of my pounding heart, and the closeness of her; and at last I reached out and my hand found her hip, and I felt the warm bend where her leg met her body. An ache rose up in me like a flame and I knew then that it had been too much to ask of my simple flesh.

Hannah stiffened, cautiously, unencouraging; then, as I did not withdraw my hand, she rolled over to face me. In the filtered light of the neon motel sign through the curtain, I could just make out her features, and the somber depths of her eyes. She gave me a long, searching look, then raised her own fingertips, tentatively, to my cheek. I shivered at her touch, and turned my face into her hand.

"Ah, Jeremiah," Hannah breathed, almost sadly

"I'm sorry," I whispered, whether to her or to LeeAnne or to myself, I didn't know. There was such a fierce, sweet longing in me. I touched her hand alongside my face, and kissed her fingers, gently, breathing in the scent of her skin, feeling my desire opening out like a long exquisite fall. Hannah's fingers tightened along my cheek, her touch firming into a caress, tilting my head toward her. My hand slid up the lush curve of her hip again, beneath her T-shirt to the warm hollow at the small of her back, and she arched toward me, her knee slipping between my legs. Our lips met and the years meant nothing and I knew that I was lost, and willingly, in that moment. I loved her so, and I had so missed the sweetness of her kiss.

DAVID FREEMAN

One of Us

David Freeman is the author of A Hollywood Education, A Hollywood Life, The Last Days of Alfred Hitchcock, *and* U.S. Grant in the City. *None of these previous works prepares readers for* One of Us, *a tour de force about prewar British Egypt—a novel that is radiant, stylish, intelligent, evocative, and erotic. He lives in Los Angeles.*

I CONTINUED TO WALK ABOUT ALEXANDRIA, THOUGH BY MYSELF. Giddoes asked once or twice if he might accompany me again. I thought he was going to pester me about it, until I demurred using the wonderful Egyptian compliment of refusal, "May Allah prosper you tenfold." I became neither Giddoes nor an habitué of opium houses, though there was a change in the way I viewed Alexandria, perhaps brought on by the opium, but more likely induced by the spirit of the city. Earlier, when I had walked the streets, I felt like a tourist, and not a very imaginative one. Now I seemed to sprout antennae. Instead of earnestly looking at monuments and mosques, I felt meaning in simple things—the laundry that hangs like flags outside tenement-house windows and the tea and cakes at the cafés. A sense of elusive metaphor concentrated my mind and made me aware I was in a place that is a factory for memory. Even newly minted memories feel old here. As I walked about, I knew I was in the present with its clatter of modern, mechanical sounds, but at the same time, I felt a part of the mythological city. Alexandria keeps her secrets, but she tells them, too, inscribing ancient answers on anyone who cares to ask.

Before my opium experiment, I hadn't thought to seek out pleasures of the sort Alex is well known for. In my new spirit of adventure, I found myself wandering in Sister Street, down by the harbour, where brothels are common as tea shops in London. One didn't need an introduction or even an address. It was sufficient that I was European and looking about. There were nods and soft calls and soon enough my sensual proclivities were revealed. I might have been hesitant before indulging in Giddoes's House of Answered Prayer, but in Sister Street, I did not hold back. In airless rooms with windows that admitted no light, there were dark girls from desert villages or up from the Sudan. Their degradation enflamed me and told me of desires that could not be denied even if they couldn't always be named. I gorged on unknowable companions. There was a fierce satisfaction of the flesh, if not the spirit. There wasn't much subtlety to it. I soon saw that I wanted anonymity and compliance and both were on offer in Sister Street. I revelled in the coarseness of those foetid rooms.

Perhaps it was the vision of poor lost Ruby, of an opportunity sacrificed to the uncertainty of youth, or perhaps it was simply that the Egyptian girls were there waiting. I sprawled amidst cushions and cotton sheets as two or even three of them swarmed over me, their sweaty bodies, their abundance, at my command. I wallowed in a sea of flesh taking everything female that had ever been denied me. They would pull and push, rub and lick, shaping my flesh as if it were clay. Their ears had been pierced and decorated with tiny blue beads to ward off the evil eye. One dark shining girl wore only long strands of coloured beads that wrapped round her breasts and then hung low, drawn between her legs and bound tight round her thighs. She would spread the beads apart and make a portal for me. It never failed to put me in a frenzy.

We had no common language save for my desire. They were to do as I wanted without my so much as saying what that might be. Their task was to know what it was even if I did not. I can't say what they thought—I hardly knew what I thought. Perhaps they felt they were taking something too, beyond money that is. When I spent my time with merely one, she might whisper a few words that I believe were meant to be endearments. When there was more than one, they said nothing, each working to satisfy me in a separate way. There was rarely so much as a sigh. It felt charged of course, even delirious, and when a gramophone was playing, usually some tinny circus melody, I felt as if I were in a silent film.

ALLEGRA GOODMAN

Kaaterskill Falls

Allegra Goodman is the author of The Family Markowitz, Total Immersion, *and* Kaaterskill Falls. *She is a writer of uncommon clarity, elegance, and grace who has single-handedly crafted a new kind of Jewish novel.*

NINA WASHES THE DISHES IN THE KITCHEN. SHE RINSES OUT HER crystal goblets, while Andras sits on the porch with his *Commentary*. After a bit he puts the magazine down and walks along Maple. There is the Curtis place, the long, narrow prefabricated house, adorned with window boxes now. Next to it the Birnbaums' house stands, white and quiet without Cecil and Beatrix. It is rented for the summer to the Landauers and their five sons. Cecil is going to sell the place, but he is waiting for the right offer, and a strong dollar. Across the street he sees some of the Shulman girls in their small and leafy yard. Still wearing their Shabbes dresses, they are running in and out of the yellow bungalow with old soccer balls, swinging on the tire swing. There is Knowlton's red bungalow with its chimney still unfinished, where Stan ran out of flagstones. Kaaterskill is all the same. Andras does not take the road all the way up Mohican. He loops back toward home.

He walks back into his garden through the long grass. There are leaves scattered over the back lawn. Even some weeds. He'll pull them up tomorrow. If he did it now, it would scandalize Nina and the neighbors. Working in the garden is forbidden on Shabbes.

He walks out to his arbor of lilacs and looks at the strawberry plants that grow underneath. Firm green strawberries cover the vines. The fruit is beginning to ripen, and a few are red. Andras plucks one and eats it. The strawberry is small and tart. In a bowl with sugar, that's the way his sisters serve them to the children. His tongue loves strawberries with sugar, the sweetness crunching and then melting away. Eva would be delighted by these plants. If she were still baking, she would buy rhubarb and mix together a strawberry rhubarb filling. "This will be a good pie," she would say if she were well, and she would make pies and load up the sideboard with them. She would serve them in the evenings in the garden. Pies and mandelbrot and prune cake.

In her kitchen Eva offered him rugelach filling on her spoon. Andras had laughed at her then, his older sister offering him the raspberry-and-walnut filling as if it had powers to change or cure. Now, to his surprise, he tastes what she means. Only that it is sweet to grow strawberries, and to eat them when they are just ripe. That it is good to rest in gardens and to sit in lawn chairs, the Sabbath lasting late as the long summer day. That it is good to serve and to eat, to sit and to receive the work of the baker's hands.

Andras walks through the garden and looks at the cascading lilacs growing over their trellis. He looks at the Japanese maple and the dogwood trees. At last he walks into the house. Quietly he walks into his bedroom to change his clothes. He is startled by the shape on the bed. Nina lying there asleep. He had assumed she was still in the kitchen or on the front porch. She almost never sleeps during the day. She tired herself out from all the cooking, from entertaining his sisters. Of course, they are not the easiest women to bake for. Polite, but critical. Quick to judge. Nina must have exhausted herself yesterday preparing everything, trying to meet, even to exceed, his sisters' standards.

Andras stands and looks at Nina lying there on the bed. She is curled up with her face against the pillow and her red hair flaming out around her. He looks at her and feels how beautiful she is. He has walked and walked, trying to outwalk the impulse to join himself to his wife, young and necessarily ignorant, unknowing, and, of course, confused by his history. It is his fault, choosing and then blaming her. He has blamed her and accused her in his mind, blamed her for being young. He kneels down next to her sleeping there. He wants to speak to her. He wants to ask her forgiveness, except that it would wake her. She would wake up, and she wouldn't understand.

He only dares to watch her sleep as he kneels next to her. He only speaks to her in his mind. And because he cannot wake her, asking her to forgive him, silently he forgives her: for being well in body and in mind, for remembering without pain, for living and dreaming apart from him, in her own time.

FRAN GORDON

Paisley Girl

Fran Gordon was born in Brooklyn and divides her time between upstate New York and Manhattan, where she is director of the National Arts Club's PAGE reading series. Her debut novel, Paisley Girl, *a boldly original story of a young woman whose skin is spiraled by mast-cell leukemia, is a work of dazzling language, desperate humor and eerie power.*

"WE COULD WATCH MOVIES," HE SAYS.

He puts on Steve McQueen. I fall asleep immediately. I awake later to see Peter watching over me. I drift off again, only to awake beside a half-eaten warmed-over pizza covered with anchovies, my favorite—and Peter, awake like the night. He's turned down the volume on the set so as not to disturb me. And, except for the crashing of waves in an ongoing erosion of his beach, there is silence.

WE GO OUTSIDE TO WALK THE COAST, THE DOGS BEHIND US, THE blue ahead. It begins to rain, in an instant, we're soaked. Wind surrounds us in the downpour. Life can't be spent watching movies—or is it? We fall on each other with the urgency of the passing storm. He presses me against his stucco house. We kiss. Water streams over our mouths, a cold to quench. Plaster rubs my paisley, now made visible both by the coming day and far-off flashes of lightning that illuminate my skin like a strobe, slowing our movement or so it seems, although we stand racing, one against the other. His shadow of beard is rough on my face, it forces time against me. And so I up my velocity. I reach down for him, slide my tongue in circles around his scar, our scar, the first scar, then lower, envelop his erection. Peter pulls me back up, my mouth to his, sour to salt, and I go down once more. Again, he pulls my mouth to his; I taste anchovies, Malta. Peter strips off his pants, but leaves his shirt on. There's something pedomorphic about this—the curves of buttocks and hamstrings that peek from beneath a sodden T-shirt gives Peter the appearance of a boy-child who has played too long in the rain, and somehow lost his pants.

I press against him in protection. The tank he gave me to replace my sand-covered shift is heavy, its water-laden cotton binds me. Peter lifts it like a curtain. He breathes in my flesh, his mouth open on my unmarked breasts. Rain confuses our borders. Peter cries out. His volume is alarming; it reaches the dogs who've run inside to huddle beneath the kitchen table. Howls swirl again inside me. Outside they begin, barely audible, to surface. He kneads me in rhythm with the rain until he brings forth my battened voice, until I join him in the riot of inarticulation that is the language of longing. He keens short and abrupt, like the splatter of gunfire; my sounds come longer, calling him forth. I lead him gently to the sand, lay him on a pillow of wet garments, then climb atop. Like the last piece of a puzzle our fit gives way to a picture until now unformed—with an ease I can't believe. *Easy ways*. I see in my ecstasy how like disease desire is. Both states can insinuate themselves into a body split-second, as if, perhaps, they'd been there all along. In a hypermnesis of cells, an atavism of salt. I try to stop the state, to freeze up, to feel pain, but I can't. My cells drag me further toward pleasure, acute and unbearable in its brevity. I laugh at such helplessness. His eyes meet mine in a moment's query—then he calls out coming, and I follow, hunched over, my head in his neck, his bottom bucking, our flesh sealing and separating in slaps—like bodies applauding. *Oh Yes Oh Yes*. We cry out together in an antiphony acclaiming our union. Knowing it didn't stand a chance.

CATHI HANAUER

My Sister's Bones

Cathi Hanauer has written for magazines such as McCall's, Mademoiselle, *and* Elle. *She lives in New York City with her husband and their daughter. This excerpt is from her first novel,* My Sister's Bones, *about anorexia in suburbia.*

DOM BITES HIS LIP FROM THE INSIDE. THEN HE STANDS UP AND comes over and sits on the edge of the couch, next to me but not too close. He reaches toward me, and I close my eyes, thinking now's the time, he's finally about to kiss me. But I feel a gentle tug at my hair instead.

I open my eyes. "You had something in your hair," he says. "I got it out." But he doesn't move away, just looks at me, his eyelashes thick and dark. His amber eyes are steady on mine, the color of light caramel.

I feel myself blush under his stare. I can smell him next to me, gasoline and coffee, and I can see him under his gas station clothes—the outline of his legs, of his knee. Dirt pushed up under his nails. My heart pumps away.

But he stands up again quickly. "Well, I should do a little more work. Make yourself comfortable. There're some magazines over there. Or change the channel, if you want. I'm not watching this crap anyway." He steps back to his desk and sits again.

Now's my chance to do what I came here for, and I know if I don't take it, it might not come again. I get up, feeling like I'm in a dream, and make my way over to Dominick's chair. When I get there, I kneel down on the floor and put my palm on the crotch of his pants.

"What are you *doing*?" he says. But he doesn't sound mad, and he doesn't push my hand away.

I look down then, at my hand—I'm afraid if I see his face, I'll lose courage, or he'll try to stop me. I move my palm gently, then a little more firmly, until I feel him get hard beneath it.

For a few seconds he doesn't move, and I keep going, holding my breath, my hair in front of my face. And then he leans back and spreads his legs a little, and that's when I know he's given in, and I want to laugh with happiness, to stand up and hug him. Behind him, I catch sight of the light switch, and I reach out and flip it off, so no one outside can see in. Then I fumble with the top of his pants, but I can't get the clasp, and after a second he reaches down and helps me. I unzip, still not looking at him. His pants come open. White underwear. I move it gently, and he springs out, bigger than I expected.

Somehow I know what to do this time, and I'm so nervous—and so thrilled he's letting me do this—that I'm not grossed out when I close my mouth over him. He's breathing harder now, his chest moving in and out. His hand touches the back of my head, guiding me. I close my eyes. I'm the one in control, the one with the power. Now I see what all my friends see in this.

He moves faster and faster, pushing against the back of my

mouth, almost to my throat. I concentrate on his breathing, and his excitement keeps me going. I open my mouth wider, afraid to let my teeth touch him, and after a minute I hear him groan. And then he jerks and comes into my mouth, again and again.

I want to gag and spit it out, but I know I can't, you're supposed to swallow. I close my eyes tighter and force the stuff down my throat. It's hot and salty, almost unbearable. But only for a second, and then it's done, and a part of him, Dom Zeferelli, is inside me.

I hold him in my mouth until I feel his breath return to normal, which seems like a long time. Then I pull away and wipe my mouth on the back of my hand and look up. I'm waiting for him to pull me up and kiss me and hug me, tell me I'm the best, tell me he's been waiting for this. Tell me I'm the love of his life, or at least the love of his week.

But he stares straight ahead, not even looking at me. And then I get it. Of course he doesn't want to kiss me; who would, after what I just did? I stand up, so I'm looking down at him, towering over him. "I want to go all the way," I say, my voice confident.

He looks up at me. His eyebrows dart together, then back apart. He touches my arm and sighs. "No, you don't, hon."

Hon! I nod. "Yes, I do. I do." I fumble with the snap of my jeans. Somewhere in the back of my mind is the thought that I could get pregnant, but I push the idea out of my head.

But Dom shakes his head. "Come here, come down here." And he pulls me onto his lap, my legs straddling him. His arms come around my back, underneath my hair. And he kisses me—finally—once on the mouth. Soft, but fast.

My body relaxes. I open my mouth and move toward him again, determined to get him, to not let him get away, and he lets me this time, he kisses me longer, opening his mouth, too, letting my tongue in. His mouth is warm, a hint of cigarettes and coffee, just like I knew it would be. I touch his hair—beautiful dark—brown dirty hair. His tongue touches mine. I reach down and unzip my pants.

"What are you doing?" he mumbles into my mouth, but his breath is heavy now, and I keep on kissing him. In one quick motion, I pull my shirt out of my pants and push his hands up underneath it, and then I reach around and undo the bra clasp for him. His fingers come up under the material, his palms warm on my breasts. His touch is slightly rough, rougher than Vinnie's ever was, but I like it, I love it, because he's given in. I stand and yank my pants down to my socks and place one of his hands between my legs, against my underwear.

This is the truth: I think of the movies then, of how the girls act, and I copy it. I move my body around under his palm, pressing him to me. I close my eyes and let my breath get harder and heavier, like with Vinnie—but this time I want him to go through with it, this time I want to give in. There's something else different about this time, too: I can't really feel his hand. I mean, I can feel it there, but I'm not thinking about it, I'm thinking about him—what I'm doing to him, how I can make him want me, how I can have him. And it works. His hands start to move on their own. And then it's him doing things to me.

Somehow we get over to that grungy couch and he lies down on top of me. Both of us are still wearing shirts and shoes; my pants are gathered in a clump on one foot, and his pants are still on both his legs, but pulled down to his feet. I slide my hands up his shirt, then unbutton it and kiss his chest. He smells like sweat and a hint of scent—powder, or deodorant—and he tastes like tart oranges. I kiss his chest, sucking his skin, trying to make him crazy, and it's working, he's starting to moan and he's hard again. But he stops. "Wait a minute," he says. He gets up and hobbles toward his desk, opens a drawer, and comes back with a Trojan. I turn away while he puts it on—in case he's embarrassed, but also because it makes me feel a little sad. I had hoped he wouldn't use one. But I don't have time to be sad for long, because then he's back on me, trying to get inside. I close my eyes and help push him harder, till a knifelike pain pierces through me and I have to gasp.

But it's a joyful pain, too, because I'm the one causing it, and I know I want to. For a second I wonder if this is what Cassie feels when she refuses to eat: the power of being in control dulls the pain. But I still feel it, the pain, and I know she must, too. Cold sweat breaks out all over me. He moves faster now, and after a while he's coming again. I hold my breath, tightening my muscles, and it seems to go on forever—thirty seconds, a minute—till I think I might break.

But I don't, and somehow I even manage to relax my body a little at the end. When it's over, I lie there, the throbbing between my legs slowly fading. In the distance, I hear cars going by, and it occurs to me only now that we could have been caught, we would have, if someone had come in for gas. I open my eyes. The room is still and dark. Dom lies over me, his chest moving up and down. He's shrinking inside me now, a balloon leaking air, and I want to hold on to him. I'm aware of an odor, the musty couch and something else, the smell of sex. I look up at him, smiling.

SCOTT HEIM

Mysterious Skin

Always intelligent, always innovative, Scott Heim is one of America's most provocative young talents. His most recent works are Mysterious Skin, In Awe, *and* Saved from Drowning.

WE ENTERED HIS APARTMENT, NUMBER 703. HE SHUFFLED AROUND, turning on lights, then dimming them. I fell into a couch as if it were a pool of warm water. Somewhere, romantic music was playing. Minutes passed. I fought the urge to close my eyes. When he entered the room, I sat up and took a good look at his face. He seemed emotionless, regular, the sort of average joe that crafty policemen might stick into a criminal lineup to help a victim identify a guilty felon. "The bedroom's this way," he said.

More dimmed lights. I saw a bed, a bookshelf without books, and a single poster on the wall advertising a jazz festival, its *J* shaped like a saxophone. The guy opened a drawer. His hands moved toward my face. One held a miniature plastic spoon, its yellow and red handle molded into the shape of Ronald McDonald's grinning head. The other cupped a hill of white powder. "Snort this." I didn't want to, but I was already fucked up, and the coke looked cute, like glistening grains of sugar. I brought some to a nostril and breathed in. "Again," he said. Again.

He snorted the rest. Then he began tearing off his clothes and throwing them, arms flailing. Buttons popped; fabric stretched and ripped. He was evidently emulating scenes from various butch pornos. The polo shirt sailed past my head like a pastel pterodactyl. "Strip," he commanded. His dick had already hardened. It looked massive, an image from a joke's unfunny punch line, and it curved upward like a giant accusing finger. "Go down there, boy."

I figured I'd been lucky, considering most of the johns I'd tricked with had been older Milquetoast types who hadn't forced me to suck or get fucked. A few had simply held me in wrinkly arms, whispering crap like "You're daddy's little boy" or something equally embarrassing. Now, with me drunk and god-only-knew-how-many subway stops from home, those elementary acts had slipped away. I fell to my knees and took his dick in my mouth.

"You like that, don't you?" he said. He fucked my face. "Swallow it deep. Moan for me, let me know how good it is." That seemed sickening for some reason. He thrust it farther, its head tearing at the back of my throat. It choked me, and I winced. I let up a little, pulling my head back, and as his dick slid out I felt him spit on me. I heard the distinct pull of the phlegm from deep in his throat, the pause, and finally the cartoony "phew" as the spit hailed from his mouth. A thumb-sized blob hit my cheek.

I stood. For the first time, I was scared. For the first time, I was fathoms away from my usual helm of control.

He shoved me onto his waterbed, the sloshing as sudden and loud as if I'd been tossed into an ocean. He placed a knee on the bed, grabbed his dick, and slapped my face with it. It hit the blob of spit, and a tiny puddle splashed into my eye. "You're not finished, slut," he said, then slammed back into my mouth. I was drunk; this wasn't supposed to be happening. I imagined corkscrewing his dick from his body and tossing it through the window, into his Brighton Beach garden, seven floors below. That image should have been funny, but it wasn't.

His arm wrapped around my chest. He flipped me over in one motion, as if my body had been hollowed out. *Slosh, slosh.* "I'm going to give the slut what he needs." His thumb wriggled around in my ass crack, then punctured the hole.

I pictured the black scar on his thumbnail, now fishing around in the place where only one other person had been, so many years before. I briefly drifted back there. "Tell me you like it, Neil, tell Coach how much you like it." I'd told him so. Had that been truth, or just a stream of gibberish? "Tell me."

"No," I said. "It's going too far." My head reeled, and I hoped he could understand the garble. "This is what I don't do." I managed to squirm off the bed, my arm held out to keep him away. He lifted his knee and stood before me, eyes flashing.

The room grew quiet. In the outside hallway, I could hear footsteps, a walk breaking into a run. "You were at that place," he said. "I know what you were there for. You'll do what I tell you. That's what a slut does."

"I don't know why I was there," I said. "I really don't." The door to the adjoining room was cracked slightly, and when I peeked around his shoulder I could see a bathtub's porcelain edge. "Just wait a minute," I told him. "Let me piss. Then . . . I'll be back in a second."

I expected his meaty arm to shoot out and grab me, but it didn't. I brushed past him, made it to the bathroom, slammed the door. It had one of those old-fashioned locks, a little hook-shaped latch that fit into a silver eyehole. I fastened it and sat on the tub's edge, breathing. The drug's grains exploded through my brain. In a matter of hours, I would land in Kansas again. Calm down, I told myself. Calm *him* down. Be careful, finish, get the money

Then I heard him, trying to get in. I looked at the door. The john had wedged the end of a butter knife into the crack, and he wiggled it higher, toward the space where the latch connected door with frame. I actually felt my body tremble. The knife pushed higher, meddling closer to the latch until their silvers struck. The latch came loose, clicking back against the door. A second of silence passed. Then the door flew open, and the john came thundering in.

He's going to kill me, I thought. I imagined the thin, pliable shape of the butter knife thudding against my skin over and over, at last breaking through to razor my heart. I held up one hand to stop him. But he wasn't going to stab. Instead, he tossed the knife into the air. It made a half-revolution, and he caught it again, stepped toward me, and raised the thick handle. It smacked against my forehead. *Snap.*

I fell backward. The room spun in a blurry maelstrom, the naked john its center. I landed in the bathtub. My face was turned away from him, toward the gold circle of the drain. I saw stray beads of water, a soap bubble, a black pubic hair. "You're getting fucked whether you want it or not," his voice said, and in the cold space of the bathroom it echoed like a barbarous god's. "And I know you want it."

For a second I thought of Zeke, sprawled on his hotel bed, disease dotting his skin. This trick was much worse. I felt my legs being pulled up, slabs of meat a butcher hoists toward the gleaming hook. He maneuvered me into a failed headstand, and the side of my face slammed against the tub's bottom. Something made the sound of a walnut cracking.

The thumb pushed back into my ass. Another. Then, unmistakably, I felt him twiddling his thumbs inside me, that classic bored gesture I suddenly knew I'd never make again. The twiddling sent a warm throb deep into my stomach, and I groaned. He took that as his cue to pull my body toward his. My ass became his bull's-eye. His dick slammed against the hole, holding there, teasing it, and then my tight bud of skin gave way to it. He was inside me. "Gonna show you what that hole was made for." I tried to move my head, tried to focus on him, only saw the horrible bright white of porcelain and his head's shadow. The bathroom light crowned him with an enormous halo.

I felt skewered. His body pistoned back and forth as it had when he'd fucked my face. I moved my arm, attempting to stop even some fraction of his motion. In my position, I couldn't reach back to touch him. My hand smacked a faucet, and cold water began dribbling from the shower head, seasoning our bodies. My eyes closed. When I reopened them, I saw blood swirling toward the drain.

The shower of water enraged him, a rage I could feel shooting into my own body. "Slut," he screamed. From the corner of my eye I saw him reach toward the tub's edge; close his hand around a shampoo bottle. His arm raised, briefly obliterating the bathroom light. Then his arm came down, curving at full speed and force through the air. The bottle bashed against my head. The arm rose again. The bottle struck again. Blood squirted a red poppy onto the porcelain. Another swing. I thought, *It isn't breaking. It's shatter-*

proof. His dick stayed massive inside me. The bottle pummeled my head a fourth and fifth time. The noise it made—and I could hear it so clearly, a perfect sound rebounding through my head—was a hollow, almost soft *bup*.

The words *please stop* took form inside my mouth, but I couldn't say them. The shampoo bottle battered my cheekbone, my chin, my eye. More water needled down. He drilled farther through me, dismantling my guts, his dick seeming to lacerate whatever internal walls my body still supported. *Bup*. Pause. *Bup bup bup*. He beat me, matching his arm with the rhythm of his fucking. The bottle dropped, still not shattering, and landed next to my head. I read its label: BABY SHAMPOO. Below that, written inside a pink teardrop, NO MORE TEARS.

"God, you want it. Take that cock all the way inside there." His words blended into a moan, a yell, a kind of cough. I felt hot and gluey spurts bulleting deep inside me, bursts of wet heat, arrows aimed for the pit of my stomach. The spurts ricocheted off my body's ruined walls, staining me everywhere with their deadly graffiti, and if I opened my mouth I knew they would spew out. But my mouth was open. I was trying to scream.

I still strained to bat him away. It was too late; he had finished. He pulled his dick out and dropped my legs back into the tub.

Water streamed beside my face. My blood, a granular swirl of soap, and a stray bullet of his sperm blended into it and zoomed toward the drain. I found I could move at last, and I looked up at him. He walked out, swatting the light switch. The darkness wasn't what I needed, but it was close.

ZOË HELLER

Everything You Know

Author Zoë Heller was born in London and went to Oxford. But she also attended Columbia, wrote for The New Yorker, *and lives in Brooklyn, so we're claiming her as an American Writer for this anthology. Besides, her first novel,* Everything You Know, *manages to be not just feisty, fast, funny, and sharply satirical, but also a truly haunting story of tragedy and redemption.*

28 February 1979

I slept with a married man last night. I met him at the wine bar down the road from work. He was there on his own. Sandra from work got talking to him first, but he was giving me the eye, and when she went off to buy fags, he turned to me and said quietly, "Do you want to get out of here?" Just that, no introduction. Oh God, it was so sexy—I practically peed myself. I said I couldn't because of Sandra, so when she came back he asked her to come along too. It was really freezing out but he made us walk for ages. He is quite a bit older (thirty-five???) and no oil painting, but for some reason I was into it. I think I like them older and a bit ugly. I get fearful and inhibited in the presence of someone too good-looking. Good to be the golden young princess surrendering to a pockmarked old tyrant. Sandra got annoyed at being the gooseberry after a bit and got a taxi home. We carried on walking. Smoked a joint. We talked about everything—he's called Michael, he works in marketing and he lives in Chiswick with his wife and two kids. I said didn't his wife mind him wandering around late at night with strange girls? And he looked at me funnily and said it wasn't like that and I had to learn about marriage. He was very ironic and cool. When I told him I wanted to train in aromatherapy, he laughed and said didn't I have anything better to do with my time? Finally, when I was about to pass out, we got a cab and went to Soho—to some drinking club—dirty and sad with a lot of very pissed old guys. We sat in the back and he ordered vodka gimlets for us—which he said is the only cocktail worth drinking. By this point, I was knackered and must have looked like shit. But then he asked me where I lived and could we go there? I truly didn't want to sleep with him because I was so tired and feeling so ugly and worn-out and I couldn't really imagine him at the squat. I smiled in this very calm way and said, "Oh Michael, let's not. It wouldn't be wise." He just looked at me and laughed. At first I was pissed off but then I started laughing too. This terrible passivity came over me and I thought, well, it's going to happen, so why fight it? We got a taxi here. I told him he had to be quiet because of the other people in the house, but he didn't take any notice. Why do you live in such a shitty place? he said when we got inside. Is this your experiment in seeing how the other half live? I hadn't taken the key out of the front door and he had his hands on my breasts. He pulled my shirt over my head and then he undid my bra. I kept thinking Marcus or Lydia was going to walk out and find us, plus I felt ridiculous standing there in the hallway with no top on, but he refused to stop. He undressed me completely—unzipped my jeans, pulled them down around my ankles. He laughed and said "Good girl" when he saw I had no knickers on. Then he knelt down, took my shoes and socks off and—to my horror—kissed each of my toes. He licked me like a cat from my ankles all the way up the inside of my thighs. I'm leaning against the front door, unbelievably embarrassed and turned on. I'm thinking JESUS CHRIST. He's still completely dressed, which is freaking me out, but he won't let me undo anything. He asks me where the bedroom is and I point and he says, Let's go, and then I have to walk in front of him upstairs into the bedroom with him staring at my arse, and just as I'm thinking Thank God the lights are off, he starts flicking them on. In the corridor, and then in the bedroom. He looks around and I think he is going to say something mean about it but he doesn't—his eyes are half closed and he's just looking and looking at me, drinking me in, and it's like he's in the sex zone or something. I tried again to undress him but he wouldn't let me. He pushed me on the bed and then he undressed himself while I watched. He was very very beautiful, like a wrestling angel. A small, tough, brown body, with dark, soft hair on the chest. He wasn't wearing underpants either. His penis was very erect and the most vivid fuchsia. Then he pushed my legs apart and licked me. He did this for a long time and kept looking up at me. At first I was sick with self-consciousness, but the way he did it, after a while I didn't care. Then he started fucking me. I'm getting wet just thinking about it. I knew I wasn't going to come, so I faked. When he was done, he held me tight and kissed me all over my face. We drifted off for a bit—just the most gorgeous, warm soft snooze, and then a little later, I woke to find him licking me all over again—like I was some incredibly delicious chocolate. He left at about four in the morning—God knows what he told his wife—and I drifted off into a lovely, postfuck sleep. This morning I woke with a terrible hangover—head clanging like the alarm at a railway crossing, the room all thick with the smell of fucking. I should feel terrible about it but don't—just exhilarated and wanting to see him again. I think he will call. He was very cool and collected when he left but in that way that men are when they are ashamed to reveal enthusiasm.

GISH JEN

Typical American

Gish Jen grew up in Scarsdale, New York. Her work has appeared in The Atlantic Monthly, The New Yorker, *and* Best American Short Stories *of 1988 and of 1995. Among other awards she has received grants from the National Endowment for the Arts, The James Michener/Copernicus Society, The Bunting Institute, and the Massachusetts Artists' Foundation. She is the author of two novels,* Typical American *and* Mona in the Promised Land. *She lives in Cambridge, Massachusetts, with her husband and her son.*

THE CENSURE OF HER FAMILY WAS LIKE A HARD SHELL UNDER WHICH she found a certain freedom. One day—after how long?—she finally let Old Chao kiss her. This brought pleasure. And with pleasure, its on-and-off companion, regret. All her years, it seemed to her now, she had stood against life. She had studied it; she had made forays into it; but mostly she had stood by while others braved the field. Did she love Old Chao? She didn't know how to love anyone—though she did believe he loved her, that he found her a doctor for his many ailments, both those he could name and those he could not. She believed he would go on as they had, indefinitely. Yet now, in repayment for his love, in hope of finding a return love for him, she allowed him more. Then more still, surprised at how soft his lips were as he pressed them up and down her neck. She was surprised that the wet point of his tongue at her ear could make her whole body shiver, as though with fever. The firmness of his touch surprised her, too, and how many parts of her body could be cupped, and what bursting tenderness was this in her nipples? She found she liked roughness and gentleness both, and that kissing back made her tingle more; and that when the time to stop came, she ached. One day he eased her back until she was leaning on the arm of the sofa, and then he scooped her ankles up. She stiffened, afraid he was going to rape her. But he didn't rape her. He simply lay down, clothed, on top of her. She could feel his legs along the length of hers, how his continued on. He was heavy; she had to push her lungs to breathe. She filled her lungs, and in her concentration, almost didn't notice that Old Chao had begun moving according to the rhythm she'd set. She would not part her legs; still he thrust, a throb against her, but pushing into bone. Was this desire? She felt his, but less of her own than she had sitting up; until, almost as she thought that, he eased his body lower. He wasn't moving against bone anymore. Now she could feel him, a bulge like a pear. She relaxed, knowing it wrong to go on, but knowing it wrong, too, to stop him, to stop this rocking, rocking. She relaxed more, separating her legs ever so slightly—allowing him. Now they fit together, now they were moving together, her whole body tightening, arching.

"What are you watching?" he whispered. "Don't watch."

"Am I watching?"

"You don't have to watch," he urged. "Nothing to watch."

She closed her eyes.

LAURA KASISCHKE

Suspicious River

Laura Kasischke is the author of two collections of poems, Wild Brides, *for which she received the Bobst Award for Emerging Writers in 1992, and* Housekeeping in a Dream. *Her poems have appeared in* Poetry, The Kenyon Review, The New England Review, Ploughshares, *and other magazines. Her debut novel,* Suspicious River, *was a strikingly original work of beauty and poignancy. Her second novel,* White Bird in a Blizzard, *was published in 1999. She lives in Michigan.*

GARY JENSEN WAS SITTING ON THE HOOD OF HIS THUNDERBIRD with the heel of one boot up on the fender, smoking a cigarette. He looked up when he saw me pull in, and then he walked around his car, got in the driver's side; his face disappeared behind the glass as he slammed the car door shut, vanishing, then, into the belly of all that silver, steel, and smooth chrome flooded with sun.

I ran across the parking lot toward his Thunderbird, so much light bouncing off the car that I had to squint, even with my hand like a visor at my forehead, clutching the red vinyl purse against my stomach with the other hand while I ran. I pulled open the door like a big steel wing, and I slipped into the passenger's side beneath it, next to him.

He'd already started the car. "You're late," he said.

He looked perfect, a little slouched at the wheel like a man with supple bones and no worries. Blue work shirt and jeans. The brass buckle of his belt was dull, but glinting. He smiled with half his mouth, and it was sexy and lean.

Until that moment I'd never felt the need to stare at a man the way men seemed to need to stare at women—women on the glossy covers of magazines, their hips thrust forward and their slick mouths open, or on billboards—women peering suggestively out of television sets while husbands in their armchairs tried not to stare in front of their wives, but did. At the drugstore, those men would be lined up around the magazine rack all day, thumbing through slippery pages of women they'd never meet, never touch, whose voices and names they'd never hear: flattened, one-dimensional women who fingered their own nipples and stared back at the nothing. The oblivion ahead of them. Splayed, those women were just angles and lines and light against shadow, and, looking at them myself, I'd remember reading in a social studies book in high school about some lost and primitive tribe who wouldn't let the white man photograph them, who believed their souls were snatched by cameras.

These women were proof of that, I thought: The world was nothing but a fake backdrop, as if nothing before or behind them had ever existed, or ever would.

But when I looked at the side of Gary Jensen's face that afternoon, I suddenly knew why they stared. Gary gazed into the windshield as if I weren't beside him, and I understood in a flash how it was to want someone whether he wants you or not—just imagining, under clothes, skin, and how it would feel to press your own skin into it, and under that skin, blood—a human heart bobbing warm and soft, a carnal apple. I knew, then, that I'd want him no matter what. Even if I had to pay.

Finally, he said, "Hi," looking over his shoulder, backing up.

There was an inhalation of breeze through the car windows as we pulled out into the road, and then he touched the bare skin above my knee with the tips of his fingers and looked at my face. He smiled. "Well, don't you just look like a fine little slut this afternoon," he said.

I breathed.

I looked out the window.

I could feel blood climb my neck, and something hot and liquid seemed to laminate my lungs, like phlegm, or shame. I'd worn a short black skirt and high heels, checked myself twice in the minor before I left. Tight white blouse with black buttons. I'd felt sexy. Looking at myself in that mirror, I'd thought fleetingly, but with pleasure, of a dry, abandoned field set on fire by a homely little girl.

"Hey," he said, looking at me as I turned my face away, "I was just kidding, baby. You look fine." He squeezed my knee, higher this time. "Mighty fine."

Still, I couldn't look at him. The sky was perfectly blue through the windshield. A shock of red against it in the trees. As we passed the gas station, I caught a glimpse of a girl I'd gone to high school with—a woman now, I thought. She must've been twenty-four, by then, or twenty-three. Once, she'd been a pom-pom girl. All breasts and bleach-blond. Now she was filling up her black Pinto with gas, frowning, her face turned against the fumes. Rainbows of old oil at her feet. I thought I saw a baby strapped into a baby seat in the back of that Pinto. Its mouth was open and pink—yawning, or surprised. "*Mighty* fine," he said, lifting my hand out of my own lap and putting it on his pants, under the brass buckle, pressing it down on his erection. "Feel that?" he asked. "You must look hot, huh?" He leaned toward me as the red light changed to green and said, "Look at me, Leila," his hand still pressing against mine. The car roared when he stepped on the gas, and I looked up at him, and then he smiled. "That's my girl," he said. "That's my precious."

Gary Jensen drove straight down Main Street until we were out of Suspicious River. He kept his hand on my hand against him all the time, and I said nothing. It was just my hand. I looked down at my bare knees. Just knees. And I felt tired. When I closed my eyes I saw Rick against my lids. He was naked, a skeleton, with arms crossed over his ribs. *It's my body*, he'd said, with an authority that staggered me. The sun felt warm on my legs and in my hair.

"Leila," Gary said, "you know, you would give any man a hard-on. You know that, don't you?" He pressed my hand against it more lightly, then harder, and then he shifted a bit in his seat and moaned. "God, baby. I want your body for my own." He was breathing hard. "Baby, is it mine?"

I couldn't look at him again, but I tried to smile ahead of myself, at the sky, the tree, the speed-limit sign.

"God, Leila. What man could resist your body, baby?" He glanced at my legs and then at my face. "I bet many don't even try to, do they?"

"Do they, Leila?" Pressing my hand.

Still, I just smiled at my own blank smile in the windshield, but he was waiting.

"Do they, Leila?

"Do they?

"Do they?"

I bit my lip hard between my teeth because I couldn't smile anymore. I had no idea what my answer should be. I didn't know if he wanted my body to be everyone's body or only his. I didn't know if I should be modest or bold about my body. I wanted to please him, but I was just guessing at what would please him. A stab in the dark. I shrugged. I said, "I guess not."

It was the right answer, and I was relieved when he grinned then and said, "You got the most incredible body, Leila. There's some men might say you just look like a cheap whore, but that turns me on, Leila. Thinking of you going down on all them guys makes me hard."

I pleased him.

I looked out the window again, feeling better. We were nearly as far as Fennville, and the pine trees shivered in the breeze like poisoned arrows. Poisoned arrows, I thought. Poisoned sparrows. A huge bird circled over the highway in a funnel of air, tunneling further and further down to earth, slow as a bad idea or a sharp, black kite. He said, "You going to go down on some guys for me today, Leila?"

We pulled off the exit to Fennville, and Gary turned left, tires spewing up gravel and crunching it like jaws. I'd never been down that road before. I had no idea where we were.

Still, his hand on mine.

"Huh?" he nudged. "You know you'd like that.

"You'd like that, Leila. I know you'd like that. There's nothng wrong with liking that, baby.

"Leila? You gonna turn some tricks for me today?"

I swallowed and squinted—just dust in my left eye, or an eyelash swimming loose across the pupil, turning the world in that one eye to water.

"Answer me, Leila." He squeezed my hand so hard against him that it hurt, little bird bones. "Are you gonna, or do you want to go back?"

I shrugged again, again not sure what I should say, feeling naked and ashamed, but I tried to smile.

He pulled over then and unzipped his pants, pushed my face hard into his lap, holding on to my hair. I thought I'd cough, but I couldn't. I couldn't even taste him. I didn't even need to breathe. I was that far away, barely tethered to myself by a thin, white thread—though Gary was pushing, alive, in total control, taking over for me. I recognized my body as I hovered above it, but it wasn't my body. It was just a glimpse of someone I'd known once, changed—like the pom-pom girl at the gas station. I closed my eyes. Afterward, I wanted to be slapped, but he just kissed my numb lips softly.

It wasn't enough. I wanted to hurt, the way that blond man in 31 had slapped and dragged me back into this world. A newborn. The way Gary had, that first time, knocked me into my skin from the oblivion where I'd been—seeing stars, bloated, colorful planets, comets dematerializing as I passed back into the atmosphere, bruised, landing on his carpet in my red shoes. I wanted something to suck me into my body, knock me back to earth, make me feel. I was high, like a white moth caught in a gust of wind—helpless and thrilled at the same time, farther above my small hometown than I'd ever dreamed of being. I was too precious, too delicate and brightwinged now, too much sweetness in me, like a wedding dress on a laundry line, that moth landing in a swaying ocean of lace or a clear plastic bag of sleep, opened, sparkling in the breeze. Like Rick, all crisp bones, ready to be blown away. I wanted to plunge down into the dirt. I dug my nails into his neck, and he snapped me back by the shoulders with his hands. He didn't slap me, though I was gasping for it, bending closer. Instead, he murmured against my neck, into the curve where it met my chest, "God Leila, god, I'm falling in love with you."

My eyes stung, my heart was a poisoned sparrow. I wanted to throw myself against the windshield glass, then, like a bee, stinging and droning myself to death against the impenetrable sky. But he'd turned soft while my heart fluttered in its bloody nest. Something passed the car, and the hood of it flashed with light: It was a trailer with a white horse lashing its tail at a cloud of dust behind it.

KATHE KOJA

Kink

Kathe Koja has won the Bram Stoker Award and the Locus Award. She has written six novels: Cipher, Bad Brains, Skin, Strong Angels, Extremities, *and* Kink. *Her best work focuses on the strange edges and disorienting power of sexuality. She lives in Detroit, Michigan, with her husband and son.*

AND IN THAT POTION'S ALCHEMY I CAME TO SEE, TO BELIEVE THAT Lena, catalyst and guide, was in some way for me—just me somehow, not Sophie—the next step. Sophie the first and sweetest, yes, Sophie to save me from my aimlessness, Sophie to make me real but Lena now in some new way the step beyond, the step necessary, essential evolution through means of purest kink, past control and glad to be and only she could take me there. And faithful, all this time, not from fear, some lockstep sense of duty but because there was no one like Sophie, never anyone to compare but through Lena that nucleus of first connection, Sophie to me shown now in retrospect, magic mirror of what is to make what was come clear—the same wit, the same skewed vision, same sense of chaos at the heart where control lies not lost but abdicated, given over to the service of the fire—but now, become what my love for Sophie had made me, I was prepared to become something else, something wilder, something whose nature, whose art I could not yet understand.

And looking at others—at work, on the streets, on the stairs of our building, the whole mass of the excluded—I felt not smug but overwhelmed, lost in a kind of helpless wonder: *how can you live without this?* as if granted heat in a world of ice, world within worlds, this paradise of kink and it was everything to us, to me; it *was* me, it was where I belonged, the only place I could ever hope to be.

And although it seems assumed that ménage à trois means, is, nonstop fucking, still for us that definition lost all boundaries, failed to contain us because for us it was contained, subsumed in that greater bond; call it instead a kind of marriage, and if sex is the heart of any marriage still it is not the whole: *we* were the whole, here in this room, this bed, this hour and the notion of boundaries—where you end, where I begin—was not considered, did not hinder or truly apply because our true beginning was Lena's entrance into our bedroom, that silent courage as she lay beside Sophie to the music of my leaping heart.

And so the first time we made love as a trio—long legs drawn up, closed eyes and stroking hands—was not less momentous but less *remarkable*, it was what should happen, there were no surprises left. Although that was not completely true, was it? Because the night that they made love, each point of the triangle merging at last, that vision was for me so absorbing that my solo orgasm occurred almost as afterthought: it was all so *different*, the current and the arc, the way they paused to nuzzle, whisper, sigh, Lena's quiet laugh, Sophie's fingers soft to that narrow smile and a moment's return, the déjà vu of my drunken dream: Lena and Sophie in party clothes, my own rapt frustrated gaze but this, oh this was nothing like that, heat to that light, light to that darkness and when they had done they turned to me, opened their arms to take me into their heat, share with me everything they had shared with one another because now no act could be complete until it was completed by all.

And still in that intensity—of giving, of guiding—Lena showed us new ways of giving to one another, new ways to play: not so much new positions (although I was—admit it—slightly jealous to see Sophie try things so readily for Lena that she would not, had not tried for me alone: "I thought that made your back hurt?" and her sleepy smile: "Not *this* way") but a new attitude, a languor, a time-out-of-time feeling as if we stretched the time around us to accommodate our play, our passion, our lust: that's an old-fashioned word, isn't it? Lena loved it. *Lust*: not the tame sweetness of making love or the animal grunt of fucking, but somehow both and somewhere in between, the limitless hunger that can never be fully fed, only appeased for now, for today with this body, this touch, this heat, this cry: and slumber then in that vast fulfillment, satisfaction replete, to wake again as eager and as hungry as before.

It was a hunger I knew best served in trio, as now those times we spent apart seemed to wear a kind of resonance they had not had before, waked into being a worming thread of jealousy: like last night, after-work trudge into a dark apartment, no food, no them and "Where were you?" when at last they entered, snow-damp and glistening, peeling off gloves and boots and "I *told* you," Sophie's kiss, "shopping. We left you a note," pointing at some scrap, pink curl of paper unseen, and see now Lena's slowest smile, sliding hands, cold hands down my pants, tweaking at belly and balls and "You could have come with us," her cold nose against my cheek. "We asked you, remember?"

"I don't remember anything," as Sophie's hands climbed me now, Sophie's warm and open mouth and we lay there on the floor, under-door draft and their peaking nipples, cold, wriggling toes and afterward my own damp pleased inertia, lying where I was to watch their quick efficiency, sorting from the scattered clothing bra from bra, blue panties from white, long tremble of a stocking traded one to the other and for me another note in the endless anthropology, litany of comparisons in which neither was more nor less than the other but both so different, so beautifully unalike. As just now, making love: see the differing ways pleasure took them, Sophie's starfish sprawl and gulped half-sentences, Lena's silent arrowed concentration and was it imagination, my imagination or were there subtle changes when each was in my arms alone? because although our lovemaking, our lust was almost invariably practiced as a trio—not because it was wrong for Sophie and me, for Lena and me, to make love as two, but because as in everything we preferred ourselves complete—still sometimes that solar flare, the strange half-guilty glee as Lena—spread against the counter, tumbled on the couch, Lena who seemed past all experience to grow ever more desirable, as if the act of possession opened doors unglimpsed before—was in that moment only mine: and did she feel it, too? A kind of deeper focus, a fiercer, less forgiving heat? Or was it only what Sophie styled, in mingled drollery and contempt, one of those *man things*, just the simple caveman pride at having both of them to please, separately and together, mine and mine and mine alone?

DENNIS LEHANE

Darkness, Take My Hand

Dennis LeHane's first book, A Drink Before the War, *won the Shamus Award for Best First Private Eye Novel of 1994. His other books include* Darkness, Take My Hand, Gone Baby Gone, Prayers for Rain, *and* Sacred. *His work is tough, taut, and stylish—noir reinvented for the millennium. A native of Dorchester, Massachusetts, he still lives in the Boston area.*

SHE WAS WEARING A FOREST-GREEN CANVAS FIELD JACKET THAT WAS four or five sizes too big for her over a white T-shirt and blue hospital scrub pants. Usually the bangs of her short auburn hair fanned the edges of her face, but she'd obviously been running her hands through it during the last thirty hours of her shift, and her face was drawn from too little sleep and too many cups of coffee under the harsh light of the emergency room.

And she was still one of the most beautiful women I'd ever seen.

As I climbed the steps, she stood and watched me with a half smile playing on her lips and mischief in her pale eyes. When I was three steps from the top, she spread her arms wide and tilted forward like a diver on a high board.

"Catch me." She closed her eyes and fell forward.

The crush of her body against mine was so sweet it bordered on pain. She kissed me and I braced my legs as her thighs slid over my hips and her ankles crossed against the backs of my legs. I could smell her skin and feel the heat of her flesh and the tidal pull of each one of our organs and muscles and arteries hanging as if suspended beneath our separate skins. Grace's mouth came away from mine and her lips grazed my ear.

"I missed you," she whispered.

"I noticed." I kissed her throat. "How'd you escape?"

She groaned. "It finally slowed down."

"You been waiting long?"

She shook her head and her teeth nipped my collarbone before her legs unwrapped themselves from my waist and she stood in front of me, our foreheads touching.

"Where's Mae?" I said.

"Home with Annabeth. Sound asleep."

Annabeth was Grace's younger sister and live-in nanny.

"You see her?"

"Just long enough to read her a bedtime story and kiss her good night. Then she was out like a rock."

"What about you?" I said, running my hand up and down her spine. "You need sleep?"

She groaned again and nodded and her forehead hit mine.

"Ouch."

She laughed softly. "Sorry."

"You're exhausted."

She looked into my eyes. "Absolutely. More than sleep, though, I need you." She kissed me. "Deep, deep inside me. You think you can oblige me, Detective?"

"I'm a hell of an obliger, Doctor."

"I've heard that. You going to take me upstairs or are we going to put on a show for the neighbors?"

"Well . . ."

Her palm found my abdomen. "Tell me where it hurts."

"A little lower," I said.

As soon as I closed the apartment door behind me, Grace pinned me against the wall and buried her tongue in my mouth. Her left hand grasped the back of my head tightly, but her right ran over my body like a small, hungry animal. I'm usually on the perpetually hormonal side, but if I hadn't quit smoking several years ago, Grace would've put me in intensive care.

"The lady is in command tonight, I take it."

"The lady," she said, and nipped my shoulder, not very lightly, "is so horny she might have to be hosed down."

"Again," I said, "the gentleman is happy to oblige."

She stepped back and stared at me as she pulled off her jacket and tossed it somewhere into my living room. Grace wasn't a big neat freak. Then she kissed my mouth roughly and spun on her heel and started walking down my hallway.

"Where you going?" My voice was a tad hoarse.

"To your shower."

She peeled off her T-shirt as she reached the door to the bathroom. A small shaft of streetlight cut through the bedroom into the hall and slanted across the hard muscles in her back. She hung the T-shirt on the doorknob and turned to look at me, her arms crossed over her bare breasts. "You're not moving," she said.

"I'm enjoying the view," I said.

She uncrossed her arms and ran both hands through her hair, arching her back, her rib cage pressing against her skin. She met my eyes again as she kicked off her tennis shoes, then peeled off her socks. She ran her hands over her abdomen and pulled the drawstring on her scrub pants. They fell to her ankles and she stepped out of them.

"Coming out of your stupor yet?" she said.

"Oh, yeah."

She leaned against the doorjamb, hooked her thumbs in the elastic band of her black panties. She raised an eyebrow as I walked toward her, her smile a wicked thing.

"Oh, would you like to help me remove these, Detective?" I helped. I helped a lot. I'm swell at helping.

IT OCCURRED TO ME AS GRACE AND I MADE LOVE IN MY SHOWER that whenever I think of her, I think of water. We met during the wettest week of a cold and drizzly summer, and her green eyes were so pale they reminded me of winter rain, and the first time we made love, it was in the sea with the night rain bathing our bodies.

After the shower, we lay in bed, still damp, her auburn hair dark against my chest, the sounds of our lovemaking still echoing in my ears.

She had a scar the size of a thumbtack on her collarbone, the price she had paid for playing in her uncle's barn near exposed nails when she was a kid. I leaned over and kissed it.

"Mmm," she said. "Do that again."

I ran my tongue over the scar.

She hooked her leg over mine, ran the edge of her foot against my ankle. "Can a scar be erogenous?"

"I think anything can be erogenous."

Her warm palm found my abdomen, ran over the hard rubber scar tissue in the shape of a jellyfish. "What about this one?"

"Nothing erogenous about that, Grace."

"You keep evading me about it. It's obviously a burn of some sort."

"What're you—a doctor?"

She chuckled. "Allegedly." She ran her palm up between my thighs. "Tell me where it hurts, Detective."

I smiled, but I doubt it was much of one.

She rose up on her elbow and looked at me for a long time. "You don't have to tell me," she said softly.

I raised my left hand, used the backs of my fingers to brush a strand of hair off her forehead, then allowed the fingers to drop slowly down the edge of her face, along the soft warmth of her throat, and then the small, firm curve of her right breast. I grazed the nipple with my palm as I turned the hand, moved it back up to her face and pulled her down on top of me. I held her so tightly for a moment that I could hear our hearts drumming through our chests like hail falling into a bucket of water.

"My father," I said, "burned me with an iron to teach me a lesson."

"Teach you what?" she said.

"Not to play with fire."

"What?"

I shrugged. "Maybe just that he could. He was the father, I was the son. He wanted to burn me, he could burn me."

She raised her head and her eyes filled. Her fingers dug into my hair and her eyes widened and reddened as they searched mine. When she kissed me, it was hard, bruising, as if she were trying to suck my pain out.

When she pulled back, her face was wet.

"He's dead, right?"

"My father?"

She nodded.

"Oh, yeah. He's dead, Grace."

"Good," she said.

WHEN WE MADE LOVE AGAIN A FEW MINUTES LATER, IT WAS ONE of the most exquisite and disconcerting experiences of my life. Our palms flattened against each other and our forearms followed suit and at every point along my body, my flesh and bone pressed against hers. Then her thighs rose up my hips and she took me inside of her as her legs slid down the backs of mine and her heels clamped just below my knees and I felt utterly enveloped, as if I'd melted through her flesh, and our blood had joined.

She cried out and I could feel it as if it came from my own vocal cords.

"Grace," I whispered as I disappeared inside her. "Grace."

* * *

CLOSE TO SLEEP, HER LIPS FLUTTERED AGAINST MY EAR.

" 'Night," she said sleepily. " 'Night."

Her tongue slid in my ear, warm and electric.

"I love you," she mumbled.

When I opened my eyes to look at her, she was asleep.

JONATHAN LETHEM

Motherless Brooklyn

Original, inventive, stylish, and ambitious are words often used to describe the work of Jonathan Lethem. You could also add provocative, exhilarating, and unique. He is the author of five novels: Girl in Landscape, As She Climbed Across the Table, Gun with Occasional Music, Amnesty Moon, *and* Motherless Brooklyn, *which won the National Book Award. He's also written a collection of stories,* The Wall of the Sky, the Wall of the Eye. *He lives in New York City.*

SHE GROPED AT THE WALL BEHIND HER HEAD AND SWITCHED OFF the light. We were still outlined in white, Manhattan's radiation leaking in from the big room. Then she moved closer: It was a minute after twelve. Somewhere as she fit herself in beside me the cat was jostled loose and wandered ungrudgingly away.

"That's better," I said lamely, like I was reading from a script. The distance between us had narrowed, but the distance between me and me was enormous. I blinked in the half-light, looking straight ahead. Now her hand was on my thigh where the cat had been. Mirroring, I let my fingers play lightly at the parallel spot on her leg.

"Yes," she said.

"I can't seem to interest you fully in my case," I said.

"Oh, I'm interested," she said. "It's just—it's hard to talk about things that are important to you. With a new person. Everyone is so strange, don't you think?"

"I think you're right"

"So you have to trust them at first. Because everything makes sense after a while."

"So that's what you're doing with me?"

She nodded, then leaned her head against my shoulder. "But you're not asking me anything about myself."

"I'm sorry," I said, surprised. "I guess—I guess I don't know where to start."

"Well, so you see what I mean, then."

"Yes."

I didn't have to turn her face to mine to kiss her. It was already there when I turned. Her lips were small and soft and a little chapped. I'd never before kissed a woman without having had a few drinks. And I'd never kissed a woman who hadn't had a few herself. While I tasted her Kimmery drew circles on my leg with her finger, and I did the same back.

"You do everything I do," she whispered into my mouth.

"I don't really need to," I said again. "Not if we're this close." It was the truth. I was never less ticcish than this: aroused, pressing toward another's body, moving out of my own. But just as Kimmery somehow spared me ticcing aloud in conversation, now I felt free to incorporate an element of Tourette's into our groping, as though she were negotiating a new understanding between my two disgruntled brains.

"It's okay," she said. "You need a shave, though."

We kissed then, so I couldn't reply, didn't want to. I felt her press her thumb very gently against the point of my Adam's apple, a touch I couldn't exactly return. I stroked her ear and jaw instead, urging her nearer. Then her hand fell lower, and mine, too, and at that moment I felt my hand and mind lose their particularity, their pointiness, their countingness, instead become clouds of general awareness, dreamy and yielding with curiosity. My hand felt less a hand than a catcher's mitt, or Mickey Mouse's hand, something vast and blunt and soft. I didn't count her where I touched her. I conducted a general survey, took a tender sampling.

"You're excited," she breathed.

"Yes."

"It's okay."

"I know."

"I just wanted to mention it."

"Okay, yes."

She unbuttoned my pants. I fumbled with hers, with a thin sash knotted at her front for a belt. I couldn't undo it with one hand. We were breathing into one another's mouth, lips slipping together and apart, noses mashed. I found a way in around the knotted sash, untucked her shirt. I put my finger in her belly button, then found the crisp margin of her pubic hair, threaded it with a finger. She tremored and slid her knee between mine.

"You can touch me there," she said.

"I am," I said, wishing for accuracy.

"You're so excited," she said. "It's okay."

"Yes."

"It's okay. Oh, Lionel, that's okay. Don't stop, it's okay."

"Yes," I said. "It's okay." *Okay, okay:* Here was Kimmery's tic, in evidence at last. I couldn't begrudge it. I turned my whole hand, gathering her up, surrounding her. She spilled as I held her. Meanwhile she'd found the vent in my boxer shorts. I felt two fingertips contact a part of me through that window, the blind men and the elephant. I wanted and didn't want her to go on, terribly.

"You're so excited," she said again, incantatory.

"Uh." She jostled me, untangled me from my shorts and myself.

"Wow, God, Lionel you're sort of huge."

"And bent," I said, so she wouldn't have to say it.

"Is that normal?"

"I guess it's a little unusual looking." I panted, hoping to be past this moment.

"More than a little, Lionel."

"Someone—a woman once told me it was like a beer can."

"I've heard of that," said Kimmery. "But yours is, I don't know, like a beer can that's been crushed, like for recycling."

So it was for me. In my paltry history I'd never been unveiled without hearing something about it—freak shows within freak shows. Whatever Kimmery thought, it didn't keep her from freeing me from my boxer shorts and palming me, so that I felt myself aching heavily in her cool grasp. We made a circuit: mouths, knees, hands and what they held. The sensation was okay. I tried to match the rhythm of her hand with mine, failed. Kimmery's tongue lapped my chin, found my mouth again. I made a whining sound, not a part of any word. Language was destroyed. Bailey, he left town.

"It's okay to talk," she whispered.

"Uh."

"I like, um, I like it when you talk. When you make sounds."

"Okay."

"Tell me something, Lionel."

"What?"

"I mean, say something. The way you do."

I looked at her openmouthed. Her hand urged me toward an utterance that was anything but verbal. I tried to distract her the same way.

"Speak, Lionel."

"Ah." It really was all I could think to say.

She kissed me gaspingly and drew back, her look expectant.

"One Mind!" I said.

"Yes!" said Kimmery.

"*Fonebone!*" I shouted.

LYDIA LUNCH

Paradoxia: A Predator's Diary

In a more just world (hah!), Lydia Lunch would be a household name. She is a reminder that being far ahead of your time does not equal commercial success. She was writing raw, powerful, exhilarating, and totally compelling stories of New York's desperate underbelly long before it was fashionable. Her totally groundbreaking work with the seminal No Wave Band, Teenage Jesus and the Jerks, has yet to receive the audience it deserves. Her other music activities include the group Eight-Eyed Spy, her sultry cabaret singer from Planet-X persona, "Queen of Siam," plus collaborations with the Birthday Party, Roland S. Howard, Thurston Moore, Kim Gordon, and Exene Cervenka.

LIGHT A CIGARETTE, DRAG DEEP. HE'S STANDING BESIDE ME. "COME home with me . . ."

I close my eyes, whisper "Why?"

"So I can blow coke up your ass and fuck you breathless . . ."

"Get a cab . . ."

We slip into the dingy backseat of the aging yellow beast. It stinks of boozy sweat, cigarettes and chewing gum. A real aphrodisiac. I balk when my temporary distraction directs the driver to Queens. The last time, the only time, I went to Queens, I left with hallucinations of butchery and mutilation. This time, however, I was sober, not tripping on blotter, stoned on pot or drunk. Not high. Not yet . . .

The ride seems quick, the skyline of Manhattan disappearing into sunrise. And he's got my shoes off, sucking on one dainty foot while grinding the other into his full crotch. I stare out the window, blasé, not yet high, not yet turned on. He slips my shoes back on, after deeply inhaling their leathery perfume, and pays the fare, escorting me into a lush duplex. The entire apartment is done in soft creams, off-whites, ochers. Huge bay windows showcase the necropolis we just departed. We still haven't really spoken to each other. There's no reason to. Easy Latin listening swells gently around the room. He disappears into the kitchen to fix drinks, a light champagne punch. Returns with an opal tray set with delicate crystal glasses, a cocktail shaker, and small mirrored box full of finely ground cocaine. He offers a silent toast and the twinkle returns to my eyes. Perhaps just a small illumination from the mirrored box of sexual miracles he just set down and opened. He produces a petite silver coke spoon, dips it in the box, holds my chin, devouring me with his dark eyes, and places it under my left nostril. I close my eyes and sup. He repeats the ritual two or three times, never taking his eyes off my face. Infatuated with the expansion in my pupils as the blue of my eyes are erased by black. Then he helps himself. Three quick snorts up each nostril. Rubs a little on my lips. Starts to lick them. To bite them. Corners my lower lip between his canines. Draws a small ruby of blood. I can feel his heart race. Mine too. He cups my face, whispers in my ear, "Turn over, give me your ass . . ." I prop myself on the back of the soft leather, allowing him to slowly lift my skirt, slowly pull aside my panties. He leaves me there for a moment. Steps across the room, admiring his game. Returns with a small silver straw. Packs it with the white devil. Does as promised back at the club. Blows it up my ass.

Six long lines of coke later and the skin sings. Memory collapses. Time disappears. Thought is replaced with sensation. Every molecule expanding outward teleported into a parallel dimension. Breath hits pockets of pure oxygen, every pore responds, enhanced by a rush of electricity.

Entranced, slow gyrations replace apathy. I can no longer sit still. Every muscle begins to deep grind. He backs up a few feet, watching me squirm. "What do you want me to do, you horny little bitch . . . Fuck you??? Not yet . . ." He's backlit in the center of the spacious cream womb we inhabit. I can't remember his face as he stands three feet away from me, features blurred as the sun splays behind him. I'm so high I astral project. I'm watching us from somewhere beyond the ceiling. Watching him ball up his fist and strike his prick a few times. Like a drunken boxer punishing himself with slow, steady, deadly blows. I see myself, still sprawled out over the creamy couch, pulling my panties further to the side, exposing pink. We're both hypnotized. A manic edge starts to swell, swallowing us. I leave the couch and crawl on all fours, lapping at his thick fists. He continues to pound himself, slow, steady, deadly. He removes his belt, methodically cracking my ass once or twice. Asks me if I like it. I nod my head, lowering it as I raise my ass. Every time he knuckles his cock, he beats my crack, causing my pussy to quiver. I moan like a happy animal.

I return to my body. Rabid. Unleash his prick. Lick. Suck. Swallow it. Deep throat him and hold it there. Suffocating myself with musky cock. Refuse to relinquish even an inch of prick until I almost pass out. Come up for air hungry, greedy. He encircles himself in a tight fist. Beats the head against my lips, not allowing me to suck or swallow. Slapping roughly his thick, engorged meat against cheeks, allows it to rest at my nursing mouth. I suckle the tip.

He forms a noose with his belt. Slips it around my neck, sweetly pulling my hair free. Drags me crawling behind him like his favorite pet. Walks me into the kitchen. Snowy white tiles, immaculate gleam. Lifts me up unto the spotless counter which occupies center stage. Sits me facing him. Belt loosely dangling. Reaches under the counter for an industrial-size box of thick plastic wrap. Begins to encase my breasts, upper torso tightly. Wrapping and rewrapping until I'm mummified in clinging film. Cuts it off with a small sharp boning knife. Licks the edge of wrap. Seals me tight. Mechanically cuts off a large sheet. Wraps it around my face, sealing in my breath. I feel like a blowup doll ready to burst. He plants his mouth over my nose and mouth, sucking out the last of my breath. Holds his mouth over mine seconds too long. He senses my asphyxia. Lowers himself to my crotch. Sucks, bites, swallows until I come quickly, flooding his face and neck with juice. He raises up, slowly cutting a small hole between my lips. Holding the sharp blade inside my mouth until I lick and suck. He drags it out, carefully slicing a tiny paper cut on my lower lip, whose blood he's already tasted. He drinks again. A single drop. Tears the plastic from my face. I slump, sucking for air.

He pulls me to him, embracing me like a small child. Strokes my face, my hair. Pushes it from my lowered eyes. Draws them up to him. Locks in. Circles my throat with one hand. Firmly. "Come . . ." He slides me off the counter, leading me by the scruff of the neck back into the living room. Walks me to the couch, applies pressure, forcing me to kneel in front of him. Sticks his first two fingers in the mirrored box. Plants the thick white tips deeply up my nose, into my mouth, down my throat, back up my nose. Holds. Removes and savors.

I forget where I am, who I am. But know why I'm there. I turn away from him, exposing myself. Peeling damp panties over my obscene roundness. Sticking my sex straight up in the air, an overheated cougar stalking rough prey. He slinks over to me, lifting me with fat fingers coaxed into juicy cavities. Tight little holes whose greedy mouths make slurpy sounds around his digits. "You can't stand it anymore, can you . . . you need my fuck, don't you. Don't you???" he taunts.

I whisper "Yes, you fuck . . ."

He slams himself inside me. Holds me pierced on his prick. One hand scooping my throat, bending my head back, off to one side, forcing me to watch his cool evaporate. Replaced with rage, frenzied fuckface. Thrashing his head from side to side banging slim hips into round ass. Relentless delivery. Banging us both into oblivion. Throttling me with the force of his manic hammering. Every few minutes rearranging positions. From behind, on top, sideways, against the wall, straddling, bent over, on his lap, upside down, searching frantically for the smoothest, deepest route in. He puts me back on top of him, cupping my ass in magic fingers which never cease to kneed, pull, pinch, twist. Pulling me open, spreading me apart, deep bounces up and down for what seems like hours until we collapse. Both too exhausted and numb to even come. We pull apart, drenched, drained, brain-dead. "Let's go to sleep . . ." he purrs. I lie and say I'll be right in, I'd like to shower. He tells me to help myself. Disappears into the plush bedroom. I slip into the shower, its cool pulsating jets of liquid balm soothing the mauled little animal. Coming down and well spent I get dressed. Decide to leave after helping myself to a makeshift bindle. Sorry I'll never see him again. I just couldn't. Bad for my health. That cocaine.

VALERIE MARTIN

The Great Divorce

Valerie Martin was born in Missouri and raised in New Orleans. She was taught at the University of New Orleans, the University of Alabama, the University of Massachusetts, and Mount Holyoke College. She has written six novels and two short-story collections, and is probably best known for Mary Reilly, *her critically acclaimed retelling of* Dr. Jekyll and Mr. Hyde. *This excerpt is from the* The Great Divorce, *a strange, powerful novel that gives new meaning to the word "cat woman." She lives in Montague, Massachusetts, and Rome.*

AT LAST IT WAS MIDNIGHT. ELLEN THOUGHT SHE HAD NEVER BEEN so exhausted. She brushed her teeth, washed her face without looking at herself, stripped off her clothes, and climbed into the bed. It was a hot night. The air-conditioning didn't seem to do much against the heat, and Ellen had the dull thought that the compressor was going and would probably have to be replaced, at absurd expense. At some point they would have to divide the money, decide who owned the house, a thought she pushed away with such force it brought tears to her eyes. One streamed down her cheek, then another. She looked out into the darkness, through the haze of tears, her heart and head for once in unison, filled with emotions—anger, pain, fear, but most persistently a sense of intolerable sadness, so deep and so strong it seemed to press her down into the mattress. She could not move. Sleep didn't interest her; her eyes remained steadfastly open. After a long time she heard the sound of Paul moving through the house, switching out lights as he went, letting the dog in, the cat out, climbing the stairs. The bedroom door opened, and in the shaft of light from the hall he saw that she was awake and she saw that he saw it. The light went out, he entered the room, took off his clothes in the dark, and got into the bed beside her.

For a few minutes they lay still, both on their backs looking out into the room, not touching. Paul turned on his side, facing her. "You can't sleep," he said.

"No," she answered. The effort at speech produced a rush of new tears, so unnecessary as to be amusing, and she added, laughing through them, "I don't much feel like it."

He touched her shoulder tentatively, then her cheek. His fingers strayed near her lips. She had only to keep still or turn away and they would pass the few remaining hours of this night as they would pass the rest of their lives: apart. But she hadn't the strength or will to do anything but seek comfort. She caught his hand in her own, brought it to her lips, and kissed it. "Ellen," he said softly. He stroked her hair back from her face as she turned to him. His arms came around her waist, hers around his neck. She hid her face in his shoulder, which was immediately wet with tears. "I can't stand this," she said, then gave herself over to sobbing. His hands stroked her back and arms; he kissed her hair. She thought of Celia, who as a child had often come running into the house in tears, angry, outraged, and of Paul holding her stiff, unyielding little body, stroking her back and her hair, just like this, until she relaxed and the tears subsided. Ellen drew up the edge of the sheet and wiped her eyes with it. She raised her face to Paul's and found his lips with her own. His mouth opened over hers as she uncurled her legs and pressed her body against the length of his. She let one hand stray down over his shoulders, his torso, and as she did he brought his leg over hers and tightened his hands across her back. She felt an odd convulsion in his chest, a gasp in his throat. She drew her mouth away from his. She touched his cheek and found it damp with tears. "Don't cry," she said, and he laughed, for it was useless now. He held her close, her face again hidden in his chest while a racking wave of sobs washed over him. She could feel his tears in her hair. Their bodies, from long familiar habit, fit and refit against each other. Ellen kissed his shoulder, his neck, his chest, and she passed one hand down across his back, pressing him to her. When she got to his buttocks she gave a light slap, then another, and said softly, "Stop that crying." He lifted her chin to kiss her, but before he did he looked long into her face—he seemed to be memorizing it—and wiped away the last of her tears. "I will if you will," he said. Gradually they began to make love. Everything was familiar—they did not consciously move from one stage to the next—yet it was entirely new because each touch, each motion had stamped upon it the brand of the last time. Ellen felt her skin burning from his mouth and she allowed herself to be entirely open to him, in some deep unexplored core of her imagination where he was both her husband and a stranger, the beloved and the unknown. She felt greedy for his body, which he was taking from her, and he, sensing her desire, turned her this way and that, going through the long repertoire of their marriage. She wept, but asked him to go on, and she felt his tears on her breasts and back, but she said nothing, only encouraged him with her kisses and the involuntary motion of her hips.

They went on in this way for hours, falling still, silent, even asleep now and then, only to wake, one or the other, their arms and legs entwined, and begin again. The sky outside the window began to lighten, and Ellen, catching sight of it across Paul's shoulder, closed her eyes against it. A whole new surge of endless, pointless weeping overtook her. This was the morning she had never wanted to come. Minute by minute the room grew light, cool, for during the night there had been a complete change of the temperature outside; a wave of dry, cold air had rolled down over the lake and driven out the stale, hot malaise that had been hanging over the city for weeks. Though they could not feel the freshness of it in their closed room, the quality of the light was different, soft and diffuse. The objects on the dresser and the night table seemed to sparkle, mocking the agony of the couple who lay knitted together, exhausted in the tear-soaked pillows of their marriage bed. They separated their bodies a little at a time until they lay side by side, speechless, filled with dread. At last Ellen sat up and reached for the clock, turning off the unnecessary alarm. Her eyes were swollen and sore, but it did seem that they were finally dry. She turned to Paul as she got up and pulled her robe from the bedpost. "I think I understand the expression 'vale of tears' now," she said. Paul smiled weakly. His eyes were red and puffy, and his skin was pale. "Do I look as bad as you do?" she said.

"I doubt it," he replied.

ELLEN MILLER

Like Being Killed

Ellen Miller has an MFA from New York University. Her brilliant first novel, Like Being Killed, *is both utterly compelling and unexpectedly touching. Critics called her heroine, Ilyana Meyerovich (a self-described "suicidal, strung-out, psychotic Jew"), "fierce, tormented, wonderful," and "one of the most electric, highly original narrators in recent memory." She lives in New York City.*

ONE LATE-APRIL NIGHT, THE REMAINS OF PAUL'S PACKAGE AND THE two grams of coke long gone, I waited for Paul in his studio on Attorney while he was copping. Czechoslovakia, mercurial as always, was elsewhere. The dark, damp basement studio had no windows or overhead lights. Little brown nicks and holes spotted Paul's linoleum floor—scar tissue formed when he nodded out and his cigarette plopped from his slack mouth, singeing the floor. Gregor Samsa scampered over the walls and the floor and the beds with chutzpah, unhurried and unafraid for his life.

Before leaving, Paul handed me a hundred and fifty dollars from his latest scam, which he refused to describe. He asked me to hide the money. "I feel an OD coming around the corner. I'll get enough for tonight and a wake-up tomorrow. If I carry money around, I'll spend it." He counted fifty dollars from his pocket.

Fuck knows why I hid the money under Paul's mattress. I wasn't feeling creative, and in a tiny studio what were my options, really? His underwear drawer? The empty refrigerator, recently turned off by Con Ed, with no lightbulb? My hope was that simply knowing it was hidden would deter Paul from looking, even though similar tactics had never deterred me.

He returned almost an hour later, swilling a cup of coffee. "Closed."

"You couldn't find a single spot?"

"Not one."

"Did you try Flaco?"

"Yup."

"C-Low?"

"Yup."

"You're lying. You're fucked-up."

"No, baby, the spots were all closed." His voice was unctuous.

"If the spots were closed, you would have waited a lifetime until one opened. You got loaded without me."

"Would I do that to you?"

"Every time I think I know the worst about you, you surpass yourself."

"Ilyana, easy, baby." He scratched his face with both hands, rubbing, like a raccoon. "I'm telling you. Don't you trust me?"

"You're scratching. Your eyes are pinned. Your nose is running. You came home after being gone an hour with nothing. And you're trying to make me feel like a shithead for not trusting you."

"I'll go out again in a few minutes. Maybe something will have opened."

"You're a weasel."

"I'll say it once," he started dramatically, "and then I'm not saying it again. I didn't get fucked-up without you. I'm not as selfish as you seem to think I am."

"I get it. Now I'm the bad guy for accusing you of being selfish. You're good, Paul, you're good. In Mexico that's called *flipping the tortilla*."

"I didn't know you spoke Spanish. What other languages do you speak?" He started to put his jacket on, but first took a swig of coffee.

"I know exactly what you did," I said triumphantly. "You copped, then you went into a restaurant, bought coffee so they'd let you use the men's room, and you fixed up in the men's room! You're so fucking obvious."

"You're tripping, Ilyana. Tripping. I'm leaving now."

"Give me your wallet."

"Tough titties."

"Give me your wallet, motherfucker, and stop acting so pathetic."

"I don't have to prove anything to you."

"Fucking give me your wallet, Paul! Give it up!" I felt menacing and dangerous, as if I had grown six inches and gained fifty pounds of lean muscle, as I stepped toward him with my hand extended, palm up, waiting.

He remained still, and I grabbed his sleeve. He flinched, sighed dramatically, like a martyr, and turned toward the door. I charged at him and yanked his hair. He screamed and started slapping me, but the drugs impaired his balance and coordination, and he stumbled. I pinned him against the door and searched his back pockets the way Smurf had searched mine. Paul didn't resist. I grabbed his wallet from his back jeans pocket, walked backward away from him, opened the wallet. Empty. "You're an asshole, Paul."

"How do you know it's not somewhere else?"

"Empty your pockets, smart-ass." My upper lip twitched.

"Make me."

I charged at him again and pushed him against the rattling door to the studio. I pushed my hands into his front jeans pockets. Empty. I fought like a girl, pulling his hair, pinching tiny tepees of his inelastic skin wherever I could grab it, clawing his face and neck with my nails. He batted my hands away vaguely, weaving back and forth, accepting my blows like so many kisses. His nonchalance and refusal to resist fueled my fury, and now my knees, legs, and feet were involved, as I kicked him and barked his shins, screaming.

"You fucking jinxed me, you bastard! I had a thing going and you fucked me up! And now you're making me act like Nancy Spungen." I struck his nose with the heel of my palm, stunning him, but he recovered quickly and grabbed my hands, immobilizing them, recoiling from the blow to the nose.

"I didn't jinx you," he shouted, "I love you! Even when you puked and shitted all over yourself I loved you. Look at you. The shape you're in. No one else could love you like I do." *Here I go again. Same shit, different asshole.* If nothing else I had the integrity and common sense to hate myself.

I stepped back, paused, wrapped my second and third fingers around my nose, and I began, noisily, to suck my thumb.

My forehead hit the floor with a bang when he knocked me down, face-first. He twisted my arm by the elbow around my back; it hurt a lot. I concentrated on the tiny burns on the floor while I planned my next move. I lay quietly for a second, or an hour, punch-drunk, playing dead, to make him think I'd surrendered. When he loosened his grip, I flipped over, grabbed his head, and brought his face close to mine so I could scream with all the violence and volume I had, right into his ear. He jerked away from me a bit, stunned, and I took advantage of his disorientation, randomly lashing out against his body, aiming toward no particular target, with my elbows and knees and feet and fingernails. He pummeled me with his fists until he grabbed my hands again and pinned each to the floor, next to my shoulders. He couldn't hold me for long; his muscles slackened, so I wrenched free, and we wrestled some more, rolling over each other, like kids in a mutual embrace tumbling together down a grassy hill, except it wasn't fun.

Until, in a flash, I discovered that it *was* fun, lots of fun, and that he thought so, too. We released the tight grip we'd had on each other without completely letting go. Still clasped around each other, I freed Paul's arm, and he fondled his fly, his fingers fiddling with the bulging front of his jeans. The violence subsided, but we continued to cling to each other, my face in his armpit, both of us rocking slightly. Paul sang softly, like a lullaby, "Ilyana, Ilyana, Ilyana, Ilyana . . ."

My lip stopped twitching. Paul rocked me back and forth, and I calmed down, allowing him to move me gently, first in swaying motions and then more assertively toward the bed a few feet away. He kissed my neck, nibbling lightly against my jugular vein, then kissing where he had bitten, the way Bummer washed my wounded skin with her tongue after biting me. He kissed my ears and eyes and hair, and I yanked off his jacket and reached under his T-shirt to touch his concave, hairless chest.

I fingered his nipples and he gasped; Paul had a direct route of arousal between his nipples and his dick. On our rare sexual occasions, I made an effort to stimulate his tits, even though men's nipples seemed pointless and depressing. I flashed to an image of my dead friend Gerry from the night, months ago, when Margarita rubbed Vicks into his naked chest, masking the symptoms of the respiratory failure that killed him. I remember how tiny his nipples were. I remembered that he was dead, gone, still, forever. Then I flashed to an image of Susie—also bare-chested, leaning over the bathtub where I sat embarrassed one morning, almost a year and a half ago—bathing me. I remembered how enormous her nipples were: luscious, ripe, living, fleshy nipples, the opposite of Gerry's desiccated dimes, or Paul's. I remembered that she, too, was gone, differently, but equally, gone, perhaps forever.

He removed my clothes and I removed his. His skin smelled like the inside of an old, rotten refrigerator. It wasn't a body odor smell; it was moldy, fruity; it would disappear for seconds at a time and then return. Once, when I was small, I wandered into a hospital's cancer ward. The terminal patients closest to death smelled the way Paul smelled now. We put each other into our respective openings; I fellated his fingers in my mouth with my fingers up his ass. His dick was the Empire State Building. We had never responded to each other this way before. I knew he had sniffed up the dope, our dope, and couldn't taste my lips or tongue, so I applied more pressure to his numb mouth, to make him feel the force of my presence if he couldn't taste me. He asked me to scratch him, his chest, his back, his legs, his groin. My nails left little trails that were first white, then pink, then red, wherever they had been. Paul shuddered and moaned, moved over on top of me, and slowly rubbed himself against me, up and down, back and forth. We were both moist and ready. He slowly introduced himself inside, teasing, and whispered in my ear, "Shouldn't you go diaphragm yourself?"

"I guess so. I should."

"Are you going to stay here? Or do it in the bathroom?"

"Of course I'm going to do it in the bathroom. I'd never let you see me put it in. It's messy. It's embarrassing."

"Go. Go. Go. To the bathroom. Put it in."

In the bathroom, I opened the medicine cabinet above the sink where I had put the diaphragm after last using it. I washed it and applied the gunky jelly to its edges, then a blob in the middle of the cup. As always, the jelly made the thing too slippery to handle. I folded it onto itself and tried to insert it, but it jetted crazily across the room like a Frisbee, landing in the corner near the toilet. Dust and black crumbs, maybe rat turds, stuck to the jelly. At first I wasn't going to clean it; I thought I'd cram it in with all that shit on it, what the hell, but after a minute I filled the sink with water and soaked the whole mess. When the diaphragm was clean, I dried it and called out to Paul, "I'll be right there."

He didn't respond.

I applied the jelly, folded the rubber cup, grabbed it hard by the rim, and slid it in with some success, but the angle was wrong, the way the angle was often wrong when I inserted a Q-Tip into my ear canal. Pulling a diaphragm out was even harder than getting it in. I usually needed help; Susie had once stuck her hand up my cunt to pull my diaphragm out after one of my many ill-fated one-night encounters, but Paul was feeling lusty now, for the first time in aeons, and I didn't want to spoil his mood by asking for assistance with clinical, gynecological matters.

I hummed a happy little melody to myself, to the tune of childhood taunts: *I'm gonna get fucked, I'm gonna get fucked, I'm gonna get fucked.* No one, including Paul, had fucked me for the longest time. The past few weeks had been riddled with frustrations; I would get the damned diaphragm in and get fucked and fucked and fucked if it killed me. Still humming, I eyed Paul's toothbrush—or was it his roommate's?—and slid the plastic end, without bristles, inside me and angled it so that its tip would press just under the diaphragm's lip. I levered the toothbrush away from myself and with it pulled the diaphragm out. I rinsed the end of the toothbrush and put it back into its holder. Then doggedly determined to get it right this time, I squeezed the diaphragm in half, took a breath, whispered, "In. In," and shoved it inside, and it snapped precisely into place. I felt around to make sure I could finger about a quarter of the outer rim's circumference. Now I was ready, and I flicked off the bathroom light.

But Paul was gone.

The mattress was askew on its frame. The door to the apartment was open; there had been no audible slam. Still naked, diaphragm settled comfortably into its proper position, I walked to the door and closed it.

SUE MILLER

For Love

Sue Miller is the acclaimed author of The Good Mother, Inventing the Abbotts, While I Was Gone, Family Pictures, For Love, *and* The Distinguished Guest. *The* Los Angeles Times *called her "an anatomist of love in all of its guises." All of her books have been critical and commercial successes and Sue may be our most knowing chronicler of domestic life.*

THE BED WAS MADE UP WHEN THEY RETURNED, THE COVERLET REmoved, and the requisite chocolates wrapped in gold foil floated on the pressed pillowcases without making a dent. When Lottie came out of the bathroom, Jack was standing by the closet, taking off his clothes, hanging them up. She crossed the room to turn on the lamp with the scarf over it, then came back and switched off the overhead light. Just then Jack bent to pull his shorts off his long legs, his big feet. His body suddenly looked storklike and unwieldy to Lottie. How much work he had in life, living in such a body! The entire length of each articulated limb to worry about, those enormous hands and feet. She felt a rush of love for him, and remembered a passage from one of the books she'd read this summer: Edna Pontellier in *The Awakening* defending her love for

Robert, defending it on the grounds that his hair was brown, that he had a little finger permanently bent from a baseball accident. *Just so,* she thought. She ran her hand down the long, shaped muscles of Jack's buttocks. "Just so," she said aloud. He laughed.

While she peeled her clothes off, he lay back on the bed in the pinkish light. "Ah." His penis rested sideways, heavy looking, slightly stiffened, across his thigh. He gestured at the lamp. "This is as good as a boa, almost."

Lottie crawled onto the bed, bent over him on her hands and knees, took him into her mouth. After she was finished, and had lain back too, he rose up and slowly, sleepily, returned the favor. She watched him for a few moments down what seemed the long slope of her body: the shock of gray hair, the kind, worn face moving between her legs as though he wanted to nuzzle his way inside her. And then she dropped her head back and drifted away, everything eased inside her. She could feel herself flailing around, bucking, moving sideways across the bed. When they stopped, she was wedged into a corner by the headboard, her head nearly at the bed's edge. "My pink, pink Lottie," he said after a while, and she felt his breath on her, and shuddered once more.

"Oh, this is heaven, Jack. I could go on doing this forever."

"Mmm. We'll have to get a few other men in, dear."

"Let's. Let's just stay here forever, having meaningless sex."

He laughed and moved up beside her. "I love a woman who says. 'Let's,' " he said. But she thought she heard in his tone the pinch of disapproval again. He lay still next to her, not touching her. Lottie rolled to her side and turned off the light. Later she heard Jack in the bathroom, then over by the windows, closing the curtains. He came back to bed and pulled the covers over Lottie, he lay down next to her again. She listened to his breathing thicken, finally the long slow pulls of sleep. She was glad for his peacefulness; but now she was wide awake.

Meaningless sex, she had said. Why had she said that? It was not what she meant at all.

She was restless; she could have cried out or begun to sing, she felt so wild. Her hand slid down between her legs. She began a slow circling motion. She held her thighs wider apart, pressed her fingers in a smaller, tighter circle. All her muscles were tensed, her heels dug into the mattress. In the dark she bared her teeth, she gasped, she shuddered once, twice, then stopped.

When she lay quiet again, there was silence in the room. Jack's breathing had stilled to its waking rhythm. Her blood slapped in her ears. She listened, as she knew he was listening to her own breathing come slowly under control. *I won't say anything,* she thought. *There's no need to say anything about it.* And then she fell asleep.

SUSAN MINOT

Evening

Susan Minot is the author of Monkeys, Folly, Evening, *and* Lust & Other Stories. *Her writing is elegant, evocative, graceful, haunting, lyrical, and always intelligently complex. She lives in New York City.*

HE WAS RELAXED TOUCHING HER AND MUST BE USED TO GIRLS, SHE thought, and therefore he must have a girlfriend. If there was a girl she was probably a strong independent girl back in Chicago, strong-minded, a girl who made something of herself. Some great girl. But did the girl slice into him? If Ann asked and found out about a girl there was a good chance he would take his arm away, his arm which she liked having there. There was a good chance she would then step aside which she did not want to do. If she learned about some other girl it would stop the thing mounting between them, and to Ann this mounting thing felt colossal.

She ought to do something. What should she do? They were standing in the middle of the garden on the grass. Any minute he might remove his arm. She didn't want that, didn't want his arm to move away. She took hold of his hand dangling from her shoulder. Holding his hand like that felt peculiar as if someone else were doing it and after a moment she let go. There's a bench here somewhere, she said, and turned and when she turned he pulled her back toward him. Ann, he said. His other arm came up so both arms were around her and her face was close to his chest. Ann, he said over her head. Ann. The way he said her name sent a thrill through her. It was even more thrilling than the way his arms felt. Her cheek was against his shirt and she could feel the warmth of his skin through the cotton. He was running his finger under the gathered elastic of her shirt at the neck and he pulled it back and bent and kissed her skin. Wait, she smiled. What? He didn't stop and she felt his lips. They made small noises. It's just—she began, still smiling and he buried his face in her neck making her smile more. She pulled back slightly, wasn't it too fast? this is where they were supposed to be going but her heart was beating too fast. Wait, she said, and put her hand on his chest. What is it. He was not worried, he was already further than she, he was already further along. Nothing, she laughed, but do I know you? He kissed her neck, his hair brushed her face. Yes, he murmured. He pulled her up to him, You do. I do? His hair went across her lips, she reached up to touch his head and was surprised how soft his hair was. You don't mind, he said. Do you? She could not answer. A force whirled through her. Who is he, she thought as a warm languor swept through her. Who is this Harris Arden? What was the house like where he lived? What did he think of and where were the streets he walked every day. What were these arms? Who did he know and what other girls did he kiss and where did he go.

Do you know, he said, how good you feel.

His hand at the back of her neck slipped under her shirt and slipped down her back. His hand on her skin. Do you mind? he said. He was smooth, he knew how to touch. She realized it with a little contraction inside, someone so smooth might not know how much it means, his hair in her face was darker than the night, the sky was light above the trees, all of it formed around the two of them, encasing them. He was taller than Ann and needed to crouch around her and when he stood up straight he lifted her in a tight grip nearly breaking her. She felt weak, she relaxed against him, his arms held her up. She had a sudden overpowering urge to lie down.

Still it seemed fast. His arms around her were lovely, but she didn't know where she was, his hand was reaching down her spine. Harris, she said. What? His hand moved further down.

She pulled back and looked at him. His face was so close. Isn't this strange?

Is it? his fingers tidied her hair.

Yes, it's strange.

No, it's nice, he said. You're nice.

The sky was gray stone with blurred clouds and the dark hill across the water was a sleeping animal stretched out. Her sandals were wet, she felt his skin under his shirt. How long did they stand there? Around them flat shapes had no color, only shades of gray and black. He pulled her shirt down off one shoulder and then off the other and looked at her shoulders bare.

Stay like that always, he said.

He held out his jacket winglike and enveloped her in it. Ann Ann Ann, he said. She was full of words but couldn't speak, she thought without fear, where are we going? feeling her shirt off her shoulders, huddled against him, waiting, knowing there was something dangerous. He had not even kissed her mouth. She waited, protected by his coat, thinking, he is taking me somewhere, where will it be? She went along.

Other embraces came vaguely back to her. It happened involuntarily, she was not thinking of other men but they appeared, others she'd touched, conjured up by this touching, the others she'd kissed in dark city living rooms with a yellow light glowing in the sky, the ones she'd hugged at the bottom of her stoop, Frank Fallon's head was being cradled in the front seat of his car, Malcolm's arm was around her in a cab. The faces appeared alongside this swooning feeling, lips on her neck being a most particular sensation and therefore recalling the other particular feeling of other lips. The images kept coming, vague and scattered, and she thought, how could one's life keep going this way? with more and more images piling up in one's heart and crowding and swelling like music. How was one to make room and to keep all of them? The answer which Ann Lord knew now having lived a life was that one did not. Things were forgotten. An astonishing amount of what one had known simply disappeared.

RICK MOODY

Purple America

Rick Moody has written three novels: Garden State, The Ice Storm, Purple America, *and two collections of short stories,* The Ring of Brightest Angels Around Heaven *and* Demonology. *Together with Darcey Steinke, he coedited* Joyful Noise, *an anthology of contemporary writing about the New Testament. He has a completely unique and compelling vision of suburban America. This excerpt is from* Purple America, *his most recent and best novel. He lives in Brooklyn.*

—LOOK, YOU'RE NOT GOING TO TIE ME UP AND APPLY RED-HOT FIRE irons, are you? You're not going to gag me, or set the house on fire and leave me, or do any bodily harm, right? Promise?

Raitliffe pauses with a drama that unfortunately suggests to Jane Ingersoll that he's had the conversation before.—It's the only way I c-c-c-c-c—

A calculated, performative stutter.

—It's more c-c-comfortable for me this way.

—Well, then I guess it's okay. I guess it has to be okay.

So she gets to the innermost layer of Raitliffe, to Raitliffe as he is known only to selected intimates. It's the last issue to explore, the most advanced chapter in his user's manual. Or so it seems. Almost immediately he produces fuchsia velvet binds from under the pillows, bowlines one of them around the bedpost, and takes hold of her wrist. Left wrist first. A knot in name only, since she could pull it off right away. But in the spirit of adventure, she doesn't pull it off. The best she can do—because he wants her facedown—is to kick against the mattress. Emblematic resistance. Eventually, she gives this up too, gives up her feet, lets him fix the ankles. Her thighs are enough apart that she feels especially vulnerable, like he might come at her with a speculum.

—Pull a blanket over us will you?

Instead, he gives her the back rub. Some American amalgam of the disciplines of the North and the East, Asian and Netherlandish, involving both a reverence for the female body, for the luxury of curves, for the elegance of her back, thumbs probing along her spine, up under her hairline; he has a eucalyptus unguent that he pours on her. She imagines she can see it from a great height, from the ceiling, her body the way it was when she was a teenager, when she was like an ideal of beauty, in the plaid skirts of private school, ribbons in her hair, dope or stolen pills in her ridiculous patent leather purse, digits furrowing under the knots in her back, moving down to the swell of her, in cars and on living-room couches, in some epiphenomenal terrain, how Nicky gave her a back rub once before they were married, under the worst of circumstances, his dad in the hospital with a stroke, Nicky's tears upon her back, best back rub she ever had, or the music teacher in the public high school, he'd tried to give her a back rub, or a neck rub, after school, probably why she gave up the violin, the guy was a creep with horrible dandruff, or after she wrecked Kathleen's car, Kathleen's

Datsun, she had whiplash, went for physical therapy or whatever you call it, and the women there would say all the nicest stuff to her, how pretty she was as they worked on her back, though she was past pretty by then and full of worries but maybe still a little bit attractive, from which basement of reflections she emerges to notice that lips are now being gently applied to her spine, one kiss per vertebra, the twenty-first, the eighteenth, like an inchworm making its progress along her, Raitliffe climbs onto her, kisses her cheek, facing away, kisses her neck, kisses her arms, glides up to her fingers, and daintily puts the fourth finger of her left hand (loosely suspended in its velvet restraint) in his mouth, sucks on it, at which point, because he's beside her head, she can see that there is indeed some progress at last in his *primary sex organ thing*, standing out in front, well, horizontal is better than a sag—and soon he lies upon her backside, and his hands tunnel their way down under her, grab onto her breasts, so that he has secured himself, she guesses, and then he starts like he's just going to insert the thing, she reminds him to *Use protection, if you please*, and he says, *Oh, of c-c-course, sorry*, and whips out the condom, as if he has a supply of all these accoutrements, velvet ribbons, massage oil, condoms, and bourbon, it turns out, a flask from which he takes a slug, stashed underneath the bed. What other stuff must be under there? He unfurls the condom, rolls it onto himself, with a snap. Meanwhile, it's not exactly like a rain forest down there, inside of her, it's not exactly equatorial, since he hasn't been attending, so he's obliged to do preparation, lapping from behind, *You know, it's entirely possible that there might be a second noteworthy development here*, happy to report, she's falling through the cracks, murmuring vowel sounds, pulling at the velvet bonds, grinding into the sheets, when Raitliffe, athwart her, attempts to introduce the sergeant-at-arms, it fills her for a second, and then he's entirely still, bangs his head awkwardly on the upper bunk bed, seconds pass, the fullness of him, and then some infinitesimal movement, movement like no movement at all, folded into minutiae, *Come on, Come on, Come on*. How little you can get away with! He grabs her hips and works his way between them, and then stops again, still as a camouflaged bird, maybe she's getting a little dizzy, maybe there's an oxygen shortage or something, the way her face is mushed up against a foam rubber pillow, she turns the other way, not much better there, folds of the blanket impeding the passage of air. What are the symptoms of oxygen deprivation, tracers, vapor trails, halos around the lights, sudden revelations, religiosity of the Hindu, Buddhist, or Presbyterian variety? *I am inventing my own gospels, I proclaim love is about motionlessness and haste*; see, there's stuff you only learn when you are willing to be this still, until everything in you is angry, which is when Raitliffe sheathes himself again, and sighs morosely, and then nothing, she can feel condensation, tidal movement, buoys tolling, the foghorn, the tides sweeping through a narrow channel, Raitliffe pulls out of her entirely, she can't tell what's happening, he disappears off into the room, she hears the flask getting tipped over on the floor, he curses, she's grinding as best she can against the sheets, against some bunching of sheets and blankets underneath her, thinking of the moment when the straps come off, *she doesn't need Raitliffe*, with a token effort she fights against the bonds, love is change of scenery, love is the exhaustion of options, *love is the people left over*, your middle-aged eccentrics, and she says forcefully, in contralto, *Oh man*, and comes, and yanks her right hand free, to put a knuckle in her mouth, shredding the velvet ribbon, a dark shadow passes over her, no idea what Raitliffe is doing at all, except that as she travels up through the skeins of sensation, she sees that he is actually sitting on the floor watching her, *jerking off*, Raitliffe is just handling himself, desultorily, fidgeting, in a feckless retreat from the pleasures of intercourse, and when he sees that her hand is free, that she's beginning, naturally, to untie the other wrist, he gets agitated, leaps up onto her, holds down the free hand, until she gives up again, *D-d-don't move, just for a second, d-d-don't move*, and there's the sound of him doing it, holding down her one wrist with his right hand, with his left doing whatever it is he's doing, puttering, groaning, and then he clamps his hand over her mouth, not so that she can't breathe, *Shh shh*, not to frighten her, but so that she will hear his next stupendous declaration, the language of purely glandular secretions, *I love you I love you I love you I love you*. That old business, that refuge of liars. Which coincides with a sudden spattering upon her back.

TAWNI O'DELL

Back Roads

Tawni O'Dell was born and raised in the Allegheny Mountains of western Pennsylvania, which she describes as "a beautiful ruined place where the rolling hills are pitted with dead-gray mining towns like cigarette burns on a deep carpet." She earned a degree in journalism from Northwestern University. Back Roads, *her debut novel, the violent yet funny and extremely poignant tale of the confused adolescence of Harley Altmeyer, was both a critical and commercial success.*

"NO." I SAID SUDDENLY, MY FACE BURNING. "EVERYTHING'S NOT ALL right at home. Everything sucks at home."

She watched me, not with pity or curiosity or even concern. It took me a moment to figure out what it was since I had never seen it before. It was respect.

"Is there any way I can help?" she asked.

"You can fuck me again."

I almost didn't get the words out before a sob blocked my throat. She dissolved in front of me behind a blur of tears. I wiped them away with the back of my hand, then I felt the hand being pulled away from me. She placed it on her throat like she wanted me to strangle her.

I took my thumb and pressed it against the perfect black freckle in the hollow of her throat. Her hands went under my shirt and her mouth went to my mouth. Her lips, the weight of her against me made me drop my beer.

The bottle exploded when it hit the stone floor. Glass shards and beer foam sprayed everywhere. I jumped back and held up my hands in front of my face, knowing I was going to get hit and knowing there was nowhere I could hide, but I had never learned to take my punishment like a man.

Not like Misty. She always closed her eyes and tilted her head up like she was waiting for a kiss. I admired her bravery. All those times Dad dragged her off to her room, slamming the door behind him, I never heard her cry or scream.

"I'm sorry," I cried.

"It's all right," she said.

She took a step toward me. I heard the crunch of glass beneath her feet, but she kept coming. My hands were shaking. I was crying like a baby. I just wanted to go home.

She kissed me again. I felt her hands behind my neck and in my hair and her tongue in my mouth.

I thought it was going to be different this time. I wasn't hysterical tonight. I wasn't stupid with need. But it was the same. My hands crawled blindly over her body, trying to hold her, but she kept sliding through my fingers like she was made of oil.

I wasn't equipped to deal with the agony of anticipation. I wanted to be inside her. That was all I cared about. If I could be inside her, everything would be all right. I told her so.

She led me to the glass-topped table and pulled out a chair. She pushed me down into it, then slipped out of her pants. I was right.

There wasn't anything underneath. There wasn't anything under her shirt either.

She knelt down on her knees naked between my legs to unzip my fly. The soles of her feet were bloody. Like Jody's. From that piece of pipe. I had to get rid of it.

She took me in her hand and climbed on top of me.

It hadn't been real.

And guided me inside her.

Jody's feet were fine.

I did even less this time. I didn't do any of the things I had promised myself I would do if I got a second chance. I didn't look at her. I didn't pay attention to her. I didn't care if she enjoyed it. I let her ride me while I held her around the waist and felt all my rage and grief being sucked from me each time she raised and lowered her hips.

By the time we finished, she had emptied me of everything. Good and bad.

When I opened my eyes, I had the swirling galaxy feeling again. She hadn't left me this time though. She was still sitting on top of me, resting against me, with her head on my shoulder and her breasts against my Shop Rite shirt.

She kissed my neck, then my lips, and shifted in my lap. I felt myself slip out of her. She studied me like she was going over her notes and was happy with them.

"You look like you could sleep for days," she said quietly, and kissed me again. "Even in this uncomfortable chair."

She smiled and pulled back, holding me by the shoulders, still clamping my legs between her thighs. I stared dumbly at her body and wondered if I could touch her now without losing my mind.

"Come here," she said.

She crawled off me and held out a hand. I took it and held it for a moment before I could stand up.

She walked out of the kitchen, tiptoeing on the ball of one foot because she had cut her heel on the beer glass. I followed and stood in front of the glass shelves with the jungle room behind them while she bent over to fluff the pillows on the couch for me.

"Lie down," she said, patting the cushions.

I didn't move and she made a funny look with a questioning smile.

"Something wrong?"

She didn't seem to know she was naked. Or if she did, she didn't know she was beautiful. Or if she knew that too, she didn't know being naked and beautiful made her mind-numbing.

"Huh?"

"Are you okay? Come here."

She sat down on the couch. I went and sat next to her. She pushed me down gently on my back, then turned and started taking off my shoes. I was glad I hadn't worn my boots to work today after getting them wet during my trek through the woods. She probably would have thought they were stupid. Amber was right about them.

"Your foot's bleeding," I told her.

"I know," she said, glancing down at it. "I need to go put something on it. I need to clean up that mess in the kitchen too."

My fear came rushing back. I started to sit up. "I'm sorry," I said, urgently.

"It's all right."

"I'll help you clean it up."

"No." She pushed me down again and leaned over to kiss me.

I grabbed her and started kissing her back. She pulled away and told me to calm down and slow down.

"I'm sorry," I said. "I'm a rotten kisser."

"No, you're not. You just need to relax and not think about it."

She climbed over me, pushed up on all fours, and bent her head down until our mouths were almost touching, then she started running her tongue back and forth over my lips.

"I'm thinking about it again," I said, swallowing hard.

She stopped and gave me a look that was pretty close to the way I thought a woman should look at a guy if he had done a good job.

"You need to go to sleep," she told me.

"Are you coming back?"

"Yes."

I watched her limp out of the living room. She left a trail of tiny bright red drops on her gold floor.

GEORGE P. PELECANOS

Down by the River Where the Dead Men Go

More than any other writer, George P. Pelecanos has reinvented the classic noir tradition of James Cain, David Goodis, and Jim Thompson. This selection is taken from his novel Down by the River Where the Dead Men Go, *which one critic called "a rich, satisfying xydeco of alcohol, regret, murder, music, passion and place."*

AFTER DINNER, WE WALKED ACROSS MASS TO A NICE QUIET BAR IN a fancy restaurant run by friends of Lyla's. We ordered a couple of drinks—a bourbon rocks for me and a vodka tonic for Lyla—and had them slowly, listening to the recorded jazz that was a particular trademark of the house. A local politician whom Lyla had once interviewed and buried in print stopped on his way to the men's room and talked with her for a while, leaning in close to her ear, a toothy smile on his blandly handsome face. I sat on my stool and drank quietly and allowed myself to grow jealous. On the way out of the place, Lyla tripped on the steps and fell and scraped her knee on the concrete. We got into my car and I leaned forward and kissed the scrape, tasting her blood with my tongue. From that fortuitous position, I tried to work my head up under her dress. She laughed generously and pushed me away.

"Patience," she said. I mumbled something and put the car in gear.

We stopped once more that night, to have a drink on the roof of the Hotel Washington at Fifteenth and F, a corny thing to do, for sure, but lovely nonetheless, when the city is lit up at night and the view is as on time as anything ever gets. We managed to snag a deuce by the railing, and I ordered a five-dollar beer and a wine for Lyla. We caught a breeze there, and our table looked out over rooftops to the monuments and the Mall. A television personality—a smirky young man who played on a sitcom called *My Two Dads* (a show that Johnny McGinnes called *My Doo-Dads*)—and his entourage took a large table near ours, and on their way out, Lyla winged a peanut at the back of the actor's head. The missile missed its target but we got a round of applause from some people at other tables who had obviously been subjected to the show. I could have easily had a few more beers when I was done with the first, could have sat in that chair for the rest of the night, but Lyla's eyes began to look a little filmy and unfocused, and her ears had turned a brilliant shade of red. We decided to go. We drove to Lyla's apartment off Calvert Street, near the park, and made out like teenagers in her elevator on the way up to her floor. At her place, I goosed her while she tried to fit her keys to the lock and then we did an intense tongue dance and dry-humped for a while against her door, until a neighbor came out into the hall to see what the noise was all about. Inside, she pulled a bottle of white from the refrigerator, and we went directly to the bedroom. Lyla turned on her bedside lamp and pulled her dress up over her head while I removed my shirt. The sight of her—her freckled breasts, the curve of her hips, her full red bush—shortened my breath; it never failed to. She draped the dress over the lamp shade, kicked her shoes off, and walked naked across the room, the bottle in her hand. She took a long pull from the neck.

"We don't need that," I said.

Lyla pushed me onto my back on the bed and spit a mouthful of wine onto my chest. She straddled me, bent over, and began to slowly lick the wine off my nipples.

"You sure about that?" she said.

I could only grunt, and close my eyes.

LYLA'S HEAVY BREATHING WOKE ME IN THE DARKNESS. I LOOKED AT the LED readout on her clock, lay there for a half hour with my eyes open, then got out of bed, ate a couple of aspirins, and took a shower. I dressed in my clothes from the night before, made coffee, and smoked a cigarette out on her balcony.

I came back into the apartment, checked on Lyla. In the first light of dawn, her face looked drawn and gray. Her mouth was frozen open, the way she always slept off a drunk, and there was a faint wheeze in her exhale. I kissed her on the cheek and then on her lips. Her breath was stale from the wine. I brushed some hair off her forehead and left the place, locking the door behind me.

I drove straight down to the river, passed under the Sousa Bridge, turned the car around, and parked it in the clearing. No sign of a crazy black man in a brilliant blue coat. No cops, either; I guessed that, by now, the uniforms had been pulled off that particular detail.

I got out of my car, sat on its hood, and lit a cigarette. A pleasure boat pulled out of its slip and ran toward the Potomac, leaving little wake. Some gulls crossed the sky, turned black against the rising sun. I took one last drag off my cigarette and pitched it into the river.

Back in Shepherd Park, my cat waited for me on my stoop. I sat next to her and rubbed the hard scar tissue of her one empty eye socket and scratched behind her ears.

"Miss me?" I said. She rolled onto her back.

CATHLEEN SCHINE

Rameau's Niece

Cathleen Schine is the author of five novels, Alice in Bed, Rameau's Niece, The Evolution of Jane, The Love Letters, *and* To the Birdhouse. *Her books are graceful, witty, intelligent, and perceptive. She is married to the* New Yorker *film critic David Denby.*

"MARGARET," HE SAID, APPROACHING SLOWLY.

Observe and clarify through logic. He has slim, strong legs, practically hairless. Does he have them waxed or what? Why are they so tan? Observe, observe, Margaret. She stared at his thighs and then, helplessly, at his crotch. Ah, and from what I observe, I can logically deduce a great deal. This proposition really is a proposition. This is not a joke. This is no longer a joke.

He stared at her in a way she could not mistake and said her name again.

Why, we don't need uniforms, after all, she thought.

He stood before her in his Michelangelo pose, the beer bottle dangling by the neck from his slender fingers with their dentist-clean fingernails. She looked up at him, unable to speak, unable to move.

So there, Edward, she thought. You see, pleasure is a state of the soul. And to each man, that which he is said to be a lover of is pleasant. Are you pleasant to me, Dr. Lipi? As pleasant as Lily was to Edward?

She continued to stare at him, speechless and without any thought of what to do next, or even that there was a next. He looked back at her, and for a moment she thought he would begin to explain to her what they were about to do, with special emphasis on the role of teeth in foreplay. But all he said was, "Margaret, you understand me."

You? she thought. What do *you* have to do with it? It's not you I'm trying to understand.

He reached out and held her arm tightly. He took her other arm too and pulled her up. He was standing so close to the couch, to her, that she had no room to stand, no way to keep her balance. She felt his chest against her, the gym shorts hard against her. She tipped and fell back onto the couch. He stepped back and pulled her to him again.

Margaret, her face pressed against his smooth cheek, thought, Perception must be in some degree an effect of the object perceived. The object perceived is hard and muscular. The object's hands are pressing into my back. He is rolling slightly, rolling his hips, backward and forward.

He pulled off his own shirt and unbuttoned hers. His hands were on her breasts. Her flesh against his flesh. He was kissing her neck. He kissed her on the lips. This was no longer a reflection in a mirror, not a copy of which she could have only an opinion but not knowledge. This was an actual form, of which she could have knowledge.

Slipping her hand beneath the elastic waistband in the front of his shorts and running it admiringly over the form inside—a gesture to the activity of clarification—Margaret gained knowledge of it, gasped, and bit her lip.

The soul is like an eye; when resting upon that on which truth and being shine, the soul perceives and understands, and is radiant with intelligence.

But then, like an unexpected cold, damp breeze, a sudden quiver of revulsion passed through her. Dr. Lipi? Connoisseur of the curve of the lower dental arch? A droning stranger who now had his strange arms around her? What was she doing? What could she have been thinking of?

When resting not on the truth, but on a mere copy of the truth, the soul goes blinking about, and is first of one opinion and then another, and seems to have no intelligence.

So this is probably not truth, Margaret thought, pressing her lips to his neck, running her hands over his back. It can't be, can it? Pleasure, yes. But also the distinct opposite of pleasure. I hardly know this man. He's my dentist, not my lover. I am disgusted, actually, with this absurd man who has wrapped himself around me, not without encouragement, I admit, but still—if I am disgusted, and I am, then Dr. Lipi, logically speaking, cannot be the only thing desirable, can he? He cannot be truth.

"I'm sorry, Dr. Lipi." She stepped away.

Fool, she thought, looking at him in all his considerable glory. Margaret, you're a fool. Who cares if he's an idiot? And a stranger? Men sleep with idiots and strangers all the time. Yes, but I'm not a man. If Edward wants to sleep with nubile idiots with long silky hair and nearly middle-aged former-lesbian idiots with short black, tousled hair, that's his problem. Dr. Lipi, Dr. Lipi, if only the reality of you had not interfered with the idea of you, the idea of you as mere physical being. You are a mere shadow of yourself, Dr. Lipi.

"Margaret, what's wrong?" He put his hand gently on her face and stroked her cheek. "Don't clench your jaw, darling," he whispered. "Your lovely jaw."

His voice startled her. He stood before her, magnificent and now quite naked, his clothes in a puddle at his tanned feet. Oh, fool, fool. Look at this gorgeous creature, as beautiful as any statue, a man of truly heroic proportions. But statues, bless them, do not speak. And Dr. Lipi does speak. And when Dr. Lipi speaks, I remember that he and not just his perfect body and overcharged eyes exists. I remember that Dr. Lipi's personality is one of his parts.

"Margaret," he said, taking her hands and putting them on his flat stomach, then pushing them down, and then down some more.

On the other hand, she thought, "Dr. Lipi," after all, is just a name, a linguistic convenience. There is no Dr. Lipi over and above his various parts, and Margaret contemplated his various parts with increasing interest and enthusiasm.

This is not real, she thought finally. This is just an illusion of perfection. But what an illusion! She held the illusion. Dr. Lipi's hands were pushing down her jeans. The illusion was pushed between her legs.

"This is just an illusion," she said.

"Yes. It's all a wonderful dream."

SARAH SCHULMAN

Rat Bohemia

Sarah Schulman is the author of the novels Empathy, People in Trouble, After Delores, Girls, Visions and Everything, The Sophie Horowitz Story, Rat Bohemia, *and* Shimmer *as well as several works of nonfiction. She has won many awards, including Columbia University's 1973 Revson Fellowship for the Future of New York City, the American Library Association's Gay and Lesbian Book Award, and the Word Projects for AIDS/Gregory Kolovakis Memorial Award. Much of her best work takes place at the compelling juncture of provocative noirish urbanism and lesbian love story.*

WE START KISSING AND I'M LIFTING HER BODY ONTO MINE. SHE'S gorgeous. Within a few minutes I could tell from the way it was *my* hands around *her* waist and *me* lifting *her*. The way she's crawling on top of my legs, climbing on, that she was turning over to me, wanting to give up. That's one thing I knew about sex. Not sex with love, but just for the sake of it. Most people want one of two things. Either they want you to submit. Or, they want to get lost. They let you know which one it is right away. As for me, I don't have a particular sexual taste. I just like the part where she shows her desire.

When I reached down her pants and pushed inside her, this woman leaned back in my arms and said, "In this house we wear gloves."

"What?"

"In this house we wear gloves."

"What do you mean?"

"We wear latex gloves. You know, because of AIDS."

This woman had beautiful skin, like the beach, and our bodies fit. She was free and open, but not too open and she was sexy. She wanted to touch me. But I could not let her put on surgical gloves. I like to get off but I don't need to be fucked that badly.

"Well, I don't do that," I said.

"You never know," she said. "The virus is always mutating."

"I know a lot of lesbians," I said. "So do you."

She nodded.

"I've never heard of anyone who really got HIV sexually from another woman," I said.

"No, there's a case in Arkansas. My friend told me about it."

"There's probably a man or a needle lurking there somewhere," I said. "If lesbians were getting AIDS from each other, don't you think we would have noticed?"

"Better to be safe than sorry," she said.

The situation was starting to get testy.

"Look," I said. "I have an idea. You do what you want and I'll do what I want. Okay?"

So that's how it went. I fucked her and sucked her and reached behind to that place you can only get to with your fingers. Who knows what it looks like? Each time that it was my turn she held me and guided my hands to my own cunt and then held her hands over mine while I masturbated. That happened a couple of times. When she was ready to let me have it, she guided my hands there instead and put her hands over them. It was so weird, it was sexy, but there was also too much fear going on in the safest place. That place between our bodies.

I looked at this woman. I looked at her homosexuality. I watched it. I identified with her. Her nipples stood up under my fingers. Her ass fit in the palm of my hand. Her clitoris filled my mouth. Her hair was black and soft. We smoked, like lovers do, her on her back in the flashing neon light. Me, caressing her chest, smoke passing back to her and then back to me.

"This feels like a forties movie," I said. "Or a forties pickup, somewhere in Dayton, Ohio."

"Well, obviously you're the lounge singer," she said. "And I'm the New York bohemian just passing through."

"A real live bohemian?" I fluttered coquettishly. "Tell me, what's New York really like?"

"If this was the forties we'd be . . . we'd be . . ." She took another drag. "We'd be exactly who we are today. Our kind never changes. We're the international, eternal bohemia."

I put my white hand on her brown stomach. She looked like a little boy, like a Mexican film star, like flesh.

"No matter what goes on out there," she said, "we always do the same thing. We smoke pot, we have sex and we talk bullshit because we like it."

The venetian shadows flashed across her breasts.

"I know you want a drink of water," she said, holding the glass to my lips.

LESLIE SCHWARTZ

Jumping the Green

Leslie Schwartz once told an interviewer, "I am sorry to report but, in truth, I am a really boring person." I for one don't believe her. Her debut effort, Jumping the Green, *won the James Jones Literary Society Award for Best First Novel. It is a work of acute perception and deep psychological probing, powered by a daring lyricism. "Our patterns of sexual encounter are what most probably reveal our true emotional selves," says Schwartz. She lives in Los Angeles, where she is at work on her next novel.*

I STOOD UP FOR A MOMENT AND WALKED TO THE END OF MY BED, staring at the table I'd constructed entirely from the glass of car windows that had been smashed open by thieves—a project which had taken me far less time than I had anticipated because I had no problem collecting the beautiful shards of bluish glass from the cars that were broken into each night in San Francisco. I slid my hands across the surface, saddened by its fragility, and the cold seeped into me as if it were an old ragged blanket left behind on a park bench.

I crawled back into bed and as I gazed at the walls, my eyes grew heavy and in moments I felt myself falling into a dreary, leaden sleep. Hours later—the sky had darkened to night and the sound of the gutters dripping indicated that the rain had stopped—I awoke and realized I must have slept through Alice's call. I heard the unmistakable sound of boots on the stairs, then a long pause just outside my door and finally a loud knocking. I looked over at the phone and saw the insistent red blink on the message recorder. Then I heard the heavy hammering against my door again and knew who it was,

I opened it and Zeke pushed me inside, slammed me against the wall and kissed me. In moments, he had torn the shirt I was wearing in half. My jeans disappeared with the same attention to violence.

"Take away the cunt and you take away the power," he said. His breath was hot, so much hotter than my own skin that it seared my cheeks. When he spoke, he did not shout but hurled his words out in a frenzy of whispers.

"You don't like the word 'cunt.' You don't like things out of balance. But you crave them. I can see it in your eyes. Squalid, shabby thoughts behind all the lies of your modesty, your perfection, your misery."

As he spoke, he pushed his hand into me and I felt myself spilling over. I did not want him to know that he excited me but I had never been so excited and I couldn't stop my body from reacting in a way that made my head ashamed of it. The allure of it lay in the plate-smashing, cheek-slapping logic of it, how obviously it seemed to twist my body one way and come out another. To think *love* and act *fuck*, to move as if in a dream where the senses were muted but the awareness of them was not.

"Fuck you," I said, and he just slapped me across the face, just slapped me so that tears sprang to my eyes and I thought of the safe word, *cease*, but it came at me like something I could not catch, a breeze or a mist, and I let it disappear. He went to my workspace and grabbed some electrical cord. Then he tied my hands to the legs of the couch and I pictured myself years ago, dragging that couch down University Avenue and through campus to the door of my apartment, and then he was on me, forcing himself in me and at the moment he slid in, I felt a strange release, the letting go of myself. I could see my body from above, taking him in but I could barely feel it until the end when we both came in some kind of Hades of mingled breaths and sensations, our bodies merely incidental to the larger conviction that what we were doing was, in the end, not enough to shock us.

When we had finished, he immediately lit a cigarette, unleashed me and moved away. He leaned against the couch and I looked at his penis, getting smaller, gleaming with a part of me. I thought, *He just went in and stole some of me.* I had the mental image of my body getting smaller and smaller, disappearing through the opening of my vagina, of Zeke removing me from myself in that way.

"You're an amazing fuck," he said.

DINITIA SMITH

The Illusionist

Dinitia Smith has written two novels and is an Emmy Award-winning film director. She has taught creative writing at Columbia University, was a contributing editor at New York *magazine, and is a national cultural correspondent for the* New York Times. *She lives in Manhattan with her husband, historian David Nasaw, and their two sons. This excerpt is from* The Illusionist, *a haunting, heartbreaking, fiercely erotic work.*

A WEATHER BULLETIN MOVED ACROSS THE BASE OF THE SCREEN. "Winter storm warning . . . accumulations up to twenty inches . . ."

Abruptly, he turned the TV off. "Can't take it anymore! I need a blunt," he said.

"Make one for me," I said. "I want one too."

This was our language, the language we both understood. It was about sex, fuck me, let's have some dope and then we'll fuck.

He rolled the blunt, lit up, took a drag on it, then handed it to me. I moved close to him, bent down over him, and I ran the tip of my tongue along his lips, then down the side of his neck, tasting the salt of him, smelling the faint animal smell where his body's breath came up through the opening in his shirt.

As I licked him, "Oh God," he said. "This is what gets me about you. Nobody else would know you're hot like this."

I giggled, slurring it at the end. I was standing over him now, he was kissing my breasts through my T-shirt, sucking on my nipples.

"Ummmm," I said. "Nurse me, nurse me."

He pulled on my nipples with his teeth, making a vacuum with his lips, hurting me. "I'm gonna draw milk," he said, through his teeth. He buried his face between my breasts, and I was burning now.

I came to consciousness a moment, glanced at Bobby's door. He saw my look. "He's asleep," he said.

Then, in the little bedroom, can't get my pants off quick enough. He arches over me, wants to watch my face while he's got his hand inside me, wants to see me go out of control, that's his thrill. Likes to watch me, reaching his hand, his whole fist practically, deep, deep inside me.

Then, we're finished. Resting, I turn my face to him. "Now you," I say.

His hands fly to his chest. But I pin his arms back at the elbows, and when I release him, he folds them back again over his chest. I force them open again, and down flat along the side of his body.

I lift his T-shirt. His flat breasts are exposed, I can see the silky skin shining and I wet the nipples with my tongue.

At first, he's reluctant. Then his chin starts to move, side to side.

"Oh baby," I say, "trust me . . . trust me . . . I love you . . . I love you—whatever you are . . ." Wetting the smooth skin of his breasts with my tongue, circling his nipples.

His thin thighs are locked tight together. "You've never known anyone you can trust like me, baby," I murmur. "I know everything . . . yes, I do, I do . . . I *am* you. We're the same, you don't need to be afraid . . ."

And now in the dark, my hand's going slowly down his belly, as light as I can make it so he won't notice, toward the mound of his crotch. His legs are still locked tight. "Let me try," I say. "Trust me," I say. "It's our secret. We got nothing to lose, baby. Have we? We got nowhere to go but up, huh?" And I slip my hand into his jeans, and force my fingers between his legs.

This time he doesn't squeeze his legs together like he usually does, but I can't get my hand in all the way because of his jeans, the space is too tight. Pulling my hand out for a moment, I unzip his fly and he doesn't resist. And then—my fingers find him there—warm and wet and thick.

His legs relax and his thighs spread apart wider and wider and I pull the jeans down at the waist, then his Jockeys. I try to keep my fingers inside him while I do it because I'm afraid if I take them out he'll forget how good it feels and he'll close his legs up tight again. He's not wearing shoes, so it all comes right off. I'm a mother, I know how to do this, I'm used to it. Now in the dark, I can just see his dark mound, but I can't tell what it is—male . . . female . . .

Slowly, I lower myself down between his parted legs, slowly so he almost won't realize what I'm doing, and I move my face into his warm center. He lets me find him. And he lets me taste him. He's all fresh there, like cucumbers, a little salt. He lets me find the little knob with the tip of my tongue. "See, it doesn't hurt," I say. My voice is soothing, like he's my baby, don't frighten him. "Nobody'll know . . . You deserve it . . . Don't be scared . . . Don't be afraid, baby. Don't be afraid . . ." And soon our bodies are all tangled up together, and inseparable, and we can no longer tell where one of us begins and the other ends, we thrash wildly, each of us selfishly wanting it, and wanting to give it to the other at the same time and it is like we are fighting, between love and greed and love again.

JUNE SPENCE

Missing Women and Others

The stories of June Spence have appeared in The Best American Short Stories, The Southern Review, Seventeen, *and* The Oxford American. *She won the 1995 Willa Cather Award, and* Missing Women and Others *was a* New York Times *Notable Book.*

"YOU'LL NEED TO COME IN AND VISIT AWHILE," EDWINA SAID AT THE entrance to her building. She turned to face him and hooked her pinkies through his belt loops, risked a direct stare, as solid and unblinking as she dared.

There was an uncertain beat before Kyle mashed his lips onto hers, tongue scoring the roof of her mouth. He backed her into the building, and she rode his kiss up the stairs to her apartment. She did the obligatory fumbling at the lock while he lapped at the back of her neck and ears until, finally, she managed to get the door open. They lunged in.

The warm air inside, thick and dark, helped bring back that dreamy, boozy feeling. She guided Kyle to the couch and straddled him, skirt bunching up around her waist. He stroked her legs, her thighs. Snagging the nylon with his fingernail he worked a hole into the crotch of her panty hose, then eased his thumb into the opening and began gently to rub, around and around. She slid her hands along his waist and began to unbutton his jeans. He stopped stroking her, grasped her hands, and brought them behind her back. He clasped her wrists together in his fist and resumed the circular motion between her thighs. She ground her hips against him, tried to find him, but he kept his hand between them, blocking contact. She gnawed at the ridges of his ears, ran her tongue along his throat. She jabbed and suckled his lips between her teeth. She tried to free her hands, to touch him, but the grip on her wrists tightened. The thumb circles quickened, spirated inward, and she met the rhythm, turning liquid hot and cold.

Then he stopped. "Tell me what you want," he murmured in her ear. She tilted her hips against him in reply, but he wouldn't move. "No. Talk to me." She shook her wrists free.

"You know," she whispered. She raked her fingers through his hair imploringly.

"I want to hear you say it."

Only penetration, blunt and immediate, could get near the core of the thing she wanted. But she couldn't ask for that. There were other words that came close, there were ways to hint at what she wanted: *Touch this empty center; change how dead I can feel.* But she knew that as soon as she said it, the feelings would shift and elude her so she wouldn't want it anymore. Aloud would only underline what she couldn't have. She tried to kiss him instead, but he clamped his teeth shut.

"No, no," he teased. "Not until you fess up."

"Oh, I have a confession," Edwina said finally. "But I don't think you want to hear it."

Kyle gripped her buttocks eagerly. "Oh, yes I do."

"When I was sixteen," she said into his ear, low and throaty, "I was a little drugged-out slut; I didn't know what the hell was going on. There were these three guys I slept with. They were all friends. They would get me high and I would have sex with them. Separately, now; never all at once; but I didn't care which one."

Kyle's fingers crept back to the opening in her hose. Edwina continued. "Sometimes they used condoms and sometimes not. It depended on how high I was. They called me Eddie, like I was just one of the guys."

"Eddie," he murmured, and nudged a finger inside her.

"You don't want to hear the rest," she warned.

"Please, Eddie," he moaned, stabbing her with his finger.

"All right," she obliged, and rocked her hips gently. "One of these guys had his own place; he was what you'd call an emancipated minor. I stayed there sometimes, when me and my dad fought. One night he was all over my case and I said I am out of here. I went to that guy's house, the one with his own place, and the other two were there. He said I could stay as long as I wanted, I could live there, but I had to suck them all off."

Normally, Edwina would muffle a sob at this point in the telling, but she dug the heel of her hand into Kyle's crotch and felt how rigid and intent his cock was against the fabric of his jeans. Heat blossomed at the base of her spine and shuddered its way down to his finger sliding effortlessly in and out.

"This is not a sexy story," she chided, and came.

DARCEY STEINKE

Jesus Saves

Darcey Steinke is the author of three novels Up Through the Water, Suicide Blonde, *and* Jesus Saves. *Her journalism regularly appears in* Spin, Artforum, *and* The Village Voice. *With Rick Moody she coedited a collection of essays entitled* Joyful Noise: The New Testament Revisited. *She grew up in Virginia and lives in Brooklyn with her husband and daughter.*

SHE WALKED DOWN THE HALLWAY, WEARING ONLY HIS LONG BLACK Sabbath T-shirt, her swollen breasts swaying with a lush animal grace. The half bottle of red wine she found in the refrigerator and the pills she took earlier, plus a few tokes off his joint, all combined to numb out the pain in her stomach and make her weak-kneed and very high. She liked pot; it gave her a giddy sense of possibility, even hope, like warm weather in early spring or getting an unexpected large amount of money. The conversation made her dizzy too. They'd been talking like this ever since that first night at the bar in the Quonset hut out on Highway 9. She liked his Prince Valiant haircut and how he sat alone at a back table sneering at the local band. When she asked him what he did, he laughed and said cynically, *Saving the world through prayer*. The conversation that followed was the best she'd ever had, how he loved the butter-soaked Texas toast at the Western Sizzler and the tiny Graceland at the miniature-golf course on Garfield Road. He was the first person to say the new post office as well as everything else out here was ugly and she was so grateful; a few hours later she went for a ride in his car and fucked him in the backseat.

Flipping on the bathroom light, she saw a water bug run over the white Formica and disappear behind the sink. Mold spores pockmarked the shower curtain, inched up the white tile walls. The toilet was shellacked with missed piss, hairs embedded like ants stuck in amber. The room was humid, the walls swampy. Nature was taking it back. She sat on the toilet seat and reached between her legs, found the white string that hung out like a price tag, and pulled. The bloodied mouse plopped into the water and sunk down moodily to the bottom of the bowl.

She walked down the hall with her legs pressed tight, pausing in the open doorway of Steve's room. Dusk's flaxen light flooded his unmade bed and the pentacle plaque hanging above it. There was a poster of Iron Maiden, one of Blackie Lawless drinking blood out of a human skull, and a huge movie poster of a slimy seven-headed demon, each face with red ember eyes and horns the length of yardsticks. All his tapes, Krokus, Metallica, Judas Priest, were piled up by his boom box, and there was one of his pen-and-ink drawings taped up on the closet door, a surrealistic image of a saw-toothed demon with a butcher's knife in its throat and blood cascading down from its right ear into a basketball hoop, which became a spigot and flowed into a drinking glass. The caption read in big black letters: I GOT STONED AND I MISSED.

Steve worked during the week as a janitor at the hospital cleaning the operating room after surgery and, when he could get them, dealt acid and 'shrooms. Ginger felt a little afraid of him. It was easy to imagine the seven-faced dragon, between the bed and the Formica dresser, bobbing its multiple heads like thin-stemmed wildflowers frenzied in a breeze. She heard a rumor he'd poured gasoline over a dog and set it on fire and that he'd spent a year in jail for cocaine possession. Ted told her all his satanic stuff was just a joke, that none of the rumors were true. "Steve had been shitted on all his life," he said. "He's a great person, just totally misunderstood."

She walked down the hall into Ted's room, lay on the towel he spread over the sheets. A flutter of blood spilled out of her, trickled down the inside of her thighs. It always felt like more blood than it actually was. The body was weird that way, magnifying its mass and function in the mind. Ted sat on the edge of the bed. At his feet was a shoe box full of junk: screwdrivers, nails, plastic pieces from broken clocks, his old pot-leaf belt buckle. He hunched over so all she could see was his bare back, his jeans so low the crack of his rear showed. The room was drenched in smoky twilight, white light glowed from his tape player. The music was over, but the blank tape played on, a silent hum as incomprehensible as snow falling.

Moisture ran into the crack of her rear as he spread the lips of her pussy and wet his pointer finger with blood, tugged up her T-shirt, so the material gathered in folds above her bra and touched her just under the tiny bow, pressed his finger into that hollow cleft at the top of her rib cage, then swung his hand down along the curving bone. His touch left a dark line, and sent out rings of sensation like a pebble tossed into water. Sliding his hand up higher under her shirt, his fingers were cold in a sexy way, like when you first take off your underwear and your bottom is bare against a cool vinyl car seat. Pushing her bra up, he cradled a tit away from her ribs. This gave a sudden sense of her own delicateness and she shuddered. Ted undid his jeans and pushed them down to his knees. Crouching over her, butt up, balls hanging, he leaned his head down and swayed his tongue messily into her mouth, jabbed his cock against her stomach, the red skin shifting around the hard inside part.

"You're so beautiful," he turned his head so that Ginger could see the scar that made the left side of his face unrecognizable. She saw nuance, shades of red and pink lush as tapestry in his mottled face. He pushed himself inside her, suspending himself over her. Long greasy strands of hair fell forward, shadowing his features; the silver cross around his neck swung just above her eyes. She helped herself along by thinking of the girl she'd seen in a porno magazine with a shaved pussy and then of certain parts in the Manson book, how during an acid trip Jesus said to Charlie, *These are your loves and you are their need.* How he'd gone out to the family bus, filled a pan of water and given himself a whore's bath, how when the girls came in he washed their dirty feet, one by one, how the girls in turn washed the feet of their boyfriends, and how suddenly the bus was filled with naked bodies. She saw Charlie balling one girl while finger-flicking another. Ted rolled over so she could be on top, but she didn't press herself up, just clung to him. Sex was psychic. His cock inside her. Her cock inside him. Not boy. Not girl. Just frenzied protons in an electrified atom. She squinted her eyes so the light from the tape player looked like a quasar, like the big bang, like God making life out of nothing. The spirit of God hovered over the face of the water and she saw the smashed pomegranate, the figs swollen and split, honey dripping over everything. All the flesh inside her swelled with blood, tightened until it was hard to tell that they were separate. *Come into me*, she thought, and he did.

RENE STEINKE

The Fires

Rene Steinke was born in Virginia and grew up in Texas. She received an Academy of American Poets Prize. She teaches literature and creative writing at Queensborough Community College and lives with her husband in New York City. She is a cousin of Darcey Steinke. Her first novel, The Fires, *is an absolutely astonishing one-of-a-kind.*

LATER, I'D LEFT THE GATE UNLATCHED AND DIDN'T HEAR HIM COME back from his round. He tapped my shoulder, and I flinched, holding my chest. He wasn't laughing the way he usually did when he startled me. His knuckles knocked against the desktop, and he bent down to look into my face as if he were searching for something on my cheek, then kissed me between my ear and my throat.

"I think I've seen all the rooms but yours."

I couldn't have lifted my arm, and my voice flitted higher. "It's like all the other ones."

"No it's not."

When we went upstairs, something bright turned in my stomach as I unlocked the door. Inside, I went straight to the bathroom to fix my hair and pour a little bourbon into two plastic cups.

I came back, and we sat on the knobby chenille bedspread. He seemed larger and louder than he had downstairs, trying to repress the smile on his purplish lips, a scent like soap and lemons in his clothes. He glanced at my suitcases. "You haven't unpacked?"

"I just don't have anywhere to put them," I said. My sweaters were strewn on the dresser, and above it, the square mirror hung like an empty television screen waiting for something to happen. My books lay towered under the painting of the dog standing taut and noble with its ears pricked and mouth parted, listening to some high-pitched whistle. I didn't know if Paul remembered what I'd told him about my scars and, if he did, whether he imagined them as slighter than they were, the vain exaggeration of a girl trying to seem tragic. I hated that idea, and knew I wouldn't attempt to fool him. I turned off all the lights, except the tidy lamp on the bureau, and made a joke about a sloppy fat man who'd followed Paul on one of his rounds to see for himself that the hotel was safe. "Good thing he checked, right?" We laughed, and his elbow knocked against my book on the nightstand. My bosom and thighs were warmly expanding, and we were kissing again, his hand squeezing my shoulder. I wanted to talk more until I could figure out what to do. I pulled away. "I have to tell you—" He looked down at my lap and put his hand on my arm and turned it so the blistered spot faced the light. "What happened here?"

It wasn't me, I thought, *please, not me*. I shrugged and tried to smile. "Just the iron."

He put his other hand on my knee. "You have a scar here?"

I nodded. He moved his hand farther up my leg, to where the zipper began on my skirt. He spread his other hand against my stomach. "There, too," I said. He nodded and murmured something. The light seemed to flutter. He kissed me again, pulled me back onto his arms. His voice was hoarse and shaky. "Will you show me?"

The light spun and needled against the wall. I gulped down the last of my bourbon and the rest in his glass, too. I was afraid, but if I didn't do this now I'd never be able to. I'd let him see them, and then that would be it. It would be over with. If he left, I would still be okay. It wouldn't kill me.

I stood up, slipped off my stockings, and my hand shook so much it took a while to find the catch to the zipper of my skirt. It swerved as I pulled it, and when I lost my grip, the skirt fell to the floor. That was enough. I could leave my sweater on. He leaned over and traced his finger along the border of a scar on my thigh, which in the dimness looked almost natural, like a mass of freckles or the spotted colors on an animal's fur. He inhaled a breath. "You're lucky it didn't— " Then he started to say something else, but swallowed. With his head lowered, his forehead and cheeks looked extremely wide, and I noticed how clear and pale the flesh on his face was, his mouth full and open. He looked up and stared at my sweater, a pale-blue one that I thought made my neck look long and my shoulders regal. I wasn't going to take it off. He reached up and flipped the ribbed band at my waist. "Come on," he said gently, and he seemed vulnerable in his largeness, as if his body were too much for him to carry around and he badly needed my help.

Do it fast, I told myself, quickly pulling it up over my head, and the scars burst red from my torso. Sitting beside him on the bed, as casually as I could, I unhooked my bra and shrugged it off, his shirt grazing my bare arm. I was breathing so hard my chest hurt.

My body felt monstrously large, and the scars stung and rippled, the horsehead like a bad smear of blood, the pink thorns above it like claws. There were furred orangish flecks under my right breast, the rope looped on the left, but around the nipples the skin was perfect and white, like stone or velvet.

He closed his eyes, then opened them again. "So these are them," he said, stroking the marks whipping up the small of my back. He drew in closer, but I couldn't read his face. *Not pity,* I said to myself. *Curiosity is better than pity.*

His kiss was tense. I was sure he was going to leave, and I pulled back.

"You're not used to it," he said, coaxing me down to the bed so we were facing one another. His eyes were huge and dark, the lashes long and curved. "Don't be afraid."

He kissed my ear, and the stubble of his beard rubbed against my cheek, his hands puttered around my waist, then up to the first curve of my breasts. I kept thinking he would leave.

When he took off his shirt, his white skin sloped above me, his chest flecked with a few black hairs. I watched the arch of his neck, the pulse and swallow there in the paleness. The lamp on the bureau glittered. He stared down at me as if he were memorizing, going over a formula in his head that he would later recite. I kept waiting for the numbness, for that creeping sense of dislocation, like losing your hand in the dark, but it never came. The gold-white light behind his shoulder flickered, dangerous and lush.

Afterward, lying back beside him, I noticed the walls tilted at the sloped ceiling, and I felt light-headed and dizzy. When I glanced back at his face, he grimaced and turned on his stomach. "Look," he said, moving the lamp closer.

Between his shoulder blades clung thin streaks of red. The scars briared down to the small of his back, not raised, but dark and definite, almost purple, from a belt or a stick. "It's where my uncle hit me." His hands pressed flat into the mattress, the tops of his fingers whitened. I sat up and ran the side of my thumb along one of the scars, then up over the curve of his shoulder. "He was a bastard, but I didn't tell anyone. He was paying for my school." He turned over and sat up "We're the same enough, aren't we?"

ROBERT STONE

Outerbridge Reach

Robert Stone won the Faulkner Foundation Award for his first novel, A Hall of Mirrors. *He won the National Book Award for* Dog Soldiers. *He is also the author of* A Flag for Sunrise, Children of Light, Outerbridge Reach, *and* Damascus Gate. *Personally, I think he is a national treasure. He lives with his wife in Connecticut.*

She spent a cold gray afternoon trying to write. Around three she tried lighting a fire under the piece with a little Pouilly-Fuissé. It was reminiscence, about a solitary hike in Dominica she had taken one spring break years before. The island had been sumptuous, gloomy and sinister. Its mountains were shrouded in small rain. The people were secretive, their patois inscrutable. At every bend in the trail she had sensed menace and surveillance. She had done a lot of whistling in the mist on that one. Later on, others had told her about the dangers of walking alone there, but she had sensed them all along. She considered them an acceptable price for the private pleasure of the island.

Around five, she heard a car in the driveway and turned to see Strickland's van parked there. She finished the wine in her glass and waited for him to appear at the door, but for nearly fifteen minutes no one came. Just as it was dark, she heard him rap on the kitchen door that opened to the back garden. She stood up to the sight of herself in one of the hall mirrors. Its frame was gold, topped with a rampant eagle. She was wearing jodhpurs and slippers with a navy-blue shirt. She looked pale; her hair was down. She brushed a strand from her forehead.

Straight-backed, stiff-gaitedly she walked into the kitchen and saw Strickland through the glass. His graying, thinning hair was wet with rain. There were pouches under his eyes; otherwise his face was all dark angles, mean, deprived. She had never looked at him so forthrightly. She unlocked the door and stepped back and folded her arms. He came in and wiped the rain from his eyes with the arm of his sweater.

"Hi," she said coolly. "What's up?"

Strickland opened his mouth and began to speak. Words failed him. He stood in front of her, struggling with his jaw until she could stand no more of it. She put her hand out and covered his lips with her fingers. She was astonished to have done so. Having done it, she closed her eyes as though she were waiting for a wave.

As he took hold of her there was an instant when she might have hit him, caught him on the jaw with her left elbow. She very nearly did. Then there was the wet wool and warmth and the taste of his bitterness, watchfulness and humor. It turned out to be what she wanted.

"I knew you would come," she said a moment later.

"You knew it," he said. "And I knew it."

"Since when?" She could see her own face in the pane of the kitchen door as he ran his hands over her. At first she tried to make him stop by holding tight to him. It was not the way.

DAVID FOSTER WALLACE

Brief Interviews with Hideous Men

When critics write things like, "grandly ambitious, wickedly comic epic," "a sprawling piece of intellectual wizardry and social satire," and "an acidic, free-styling, 1,088-page encyclopedia of hurt," they have to be talking about Infinite Jest, *the biggest book from one of the biggest talents of America's so-called Generation X. David Foster Wallace is an endlessly inventive, exhilaratingly audacious virtuoso who has taken the concept of "weird shit" and single-handedly raised it to an American art form.*

FOR THE FIRST THREE YEARS, THE YOUNG WIFE WORRIED THAT THEIR lovemaking together was somehow hard on his thingie. The rawness and tenderness and spanked pink of the head of his thingie. The slight wince when he'd first enter her down there. The vague hot-penny taste of rawness when she took his thingie in her mouth—she seldom took him in her mouth, however; there was something about it that she felt he did not quite like.

For the first three to three and a half years of their marriage together, this wife, being young (and full of herself [she realized only later]), believed it was something about her. The problem. She worried that there was something wrong with her. With her technique in making love. Or maybe that some unusual roughness or thickness or hitch down there was hard on his thingie, and hurt it. She was aware that she liked to press her pubic bone and the base of her button against him and grind when they made love together, sometimes. She ground against him as gently as she could force herself to remember to, but she was aware that she often did it as she was moving toward having her sexual climax and sometimes forgot herself, and afterward she was often worried that she had selfishly forgotten about his thingie and might have been too hard on it.

They were a young couple and had no children, though sometimes they talked about having children, and about all the irrevocable changes and responsibilities that this would commit them to.

The wife's method of contraception was a diaphragm until she began to worry that something about the design of its rim or the way she inserted or wore it might be wrong and hurt him, might add to whatever it was about their lovemaking together that seemed hard on him. She searched his face when he entered her; she remembered to keep her eyes open and watched for the slight wince that may or may not (she realized only later, when she had some mature perspective) have actually been pleasure, may have been the same kind of revelational pleasure of coming together as close as two married bodies could come and feeling the warmth and closeness that made it so hard to keep her eyes open and senses alert to whatever she might be doing wrong.

In those early years, the wife felt that she was totally happy with the reality of their sexlife together. The husband was a great lover, and his attentiveness and sweetness and skill drove her almost mad with pleasure, the wife felt. The only negative part was her irrational worry that something was wrong with her or that she was doing something wrong that kept him from enjoying their sexlife together as much as she did. She worried that the husband was too considerate and unselfish to risk hurting her feelings by talking about whatever was wrong. He had never complained about being sore or raw, or of slightly wincing when he first entered her, or said anything other than that he loved her and totally loved her down there more than he could even say. He said that she was indescribably soft and warm and sweet down there and that entering her was indescribably great. He said she drove him half insane with passion and love when she ground against him as she was getting ready to have her sexual climax. He said nothing but generous and reassuring things about their sexlife together. He always whispered compliments to her after they had made love, and held her, and considerately regathered the bedcovers around her legs as the wife's sexual heart rate slowed and she began to feel chilly. She loved to feel her legs still tremble slightly under the cocoon of bedcovers he gently regathered around her. They also developed the intimacy of him always getting her Virginia Slims and lighting one for her after they had made love together.

The young wife felt that the husband was a simply wonderful lovemaking partner, considerate and attentive and unselfish and virile and sweet, far better than she probably deserved; and as he slept, or if he arose in the middle of the night to check on foreign markets and turned on the light in the master bathroom adjoining their bedroom and inadvertently woke her (she slept lightly in those early years, she realized later), the wife's worries as she lay awake in their bed were all about herself. Sometimes she touched herself down there while she lay awake, but it wasn't in a pleasurable way. The husband slept on his right side, facing away. He had a hard time sleeping due to career stress, and could only fall asleep in one position. Sometimes she watched him sleep. Their master bedroom had a night-light down near the baseboard. When he arose in the night she believed it was to check the status of the yen. Insomnia could cause him to drive all the way downtown to the firm in the middle of the night. There were the rupiah and the won and the baht to be monitored and checked, also. He was also in charge of the weekly chore of grocery shopping, which he habitually also performed late at night. Amazingly (she realized only later, after she had had an epiphany and rapidly matured), it had never occurred to her to check on anything.

She loved it when he gave oral sex but worried that he didn't like it as much when she reciprocated and took him in her mouth. He almost always stopped her after a short time, saying that it made him want to be inside her down there instead of in her mouth. She felt that there must be something wrong with her oral sex technique that made him not like it as much as she did, or hurt him. He had gone all the way to his sexual climax in her mouth only twice in their marriage together, and both the times had taken practically forever. Both the times took so long that her neck was stiff the next day, and she worried that he hadn't liked it even though he had said he couldn't even describe in words how much he liked it. She once gathered her nerve together and drove out to Adult World and bought a Dildo, but only to practice her oral sex technique on. She was inexperienced in this, she knew. The slight tension or distraction she thought she felt in him when she moved down the bed and took the husband's thingie in her mouth could have been nothing but her own selfish imagination; the whole problem could be just in her head, she worried. She had been tense and uncomfortable at Adult World. Except for the cashier, she had been the only female in the store, and the cashier had given her a look that she didn't think was very appropriate or professionally courteous at all, and the young wife had taken the dark plastic bag with the Dildo to her car and driven out of the crowded parking lot so fast that later she was afraid her tires might have squealed.

ACKNOWLEDGMENTS

From *As Francesca* by Martha Baer, copyright © 1997 by Martha Baer. Used by permission of Broadway Books, a division of Random House Inc.

From *Affliction* by Russell Banks. Copyright © 1989 by Russell Banks. Reprinted by permission of HarperCollins Publishers, Inc.

From *Painted Desert* by Frederick Barthelme, copyright © 1995 by Frederick Barthelme. Used by permission of Viking Penguin, a division of Penguin Putnam Inc.

From *City of Light* by Lauren Belfer, copyright © 1999 by Lauren Belfer. Used by permission of The Dial Press/Dell Publishing, a division of Random House Inc.

"Life Under Optimum Conditions," from *Seduction Theory* by Thomas Beller. Copyright © 1995 by Thomas Beller. Used by permission of W. W. Norton & Company, Inc.

From *The Girl in the Flammable Skirt* by Aimee Bender, copyright © 1998 by Aimee Bender. Used by permission of Doubleday, a division of Random House Inc.

From *My Father, Dancing* by Bliss Broyard. Copyright © 1999 by Bliss Broyard. Reprinted by permission of Alfred A. Knopf, a division of Random House Inc.

From *Waiting in Vain* by Colin Channer. Copyright © 1988 by Colin Channer. Reprinted by permission of Ballantine Books, a division of Random House Inc.

From *The Foreign Student* by Susan Choi. Copyright © 1998 by Susan Choi. Reprinted by permission of HarperCollins Publishers, Inc.

From *The Archivist* by Martha Cooley. Copyright © 1998 by Martha Cooley. By permission of Little, Brown and Company (Inc.).

From *Mao II* by Don DeLillo, copyright © 1991 by Don DeLillo. Used by permission of Viking Penguin, a division of Penguin Putnam Inc.

From *Don Juan in the Village* by Jane DeLynn. Copyright © 1990 by Jane DeLynn. Reprinted by permission of Pantheon Books, a division of Random House Inc.

From *Billy Bathgate* by E. L. Doctorow. Copyright © 1988 by E. L. Doctorow. Reprinted by permission of Random House Inc.

From *Hell-Bent Men and Their Cities* by Susan M. Dodd. Copyright © 1990 by Susan M. Dodd. Reprinted by permission of International Creative Management, Inc.

From *The Word "Desire"* by Rikki Ducornet, © 1997 by Rikki Ducornet. Reprinted by permission of Henry Holt and Company, LLC.

From *The Danish Girl* by David Ebershoff, copyright © 2000 by David Ebershoff. Used by permission of Viking Penguin, a division of Penguin Putnam Inc.

From *For the Relief of Unbearable Urges* by Nathan Englander. Copyright © 1999 by Nathan Englander. Reprinted by permission of Alfred A. Knopf, a division of Random House Inc.

From *Blues for Hannah* by Tim Farrington. Copyright © 1998 by Tim Farrington. Reprinted by permission of Crown Publishers, a division of Random House Inc.

Excerpt from *One of Us* by David Freeman. Copyright © 1998 by David Freeman. Reprinted by permission of Carroll & Graf Publishers Inc.

From *Kaaterskill Falls* by Allegra Goodman, copyright © 1998 by Allegra Goodman. Used by permission of The Dial Press/Dell Publishing, a division of Random House Inc.

From *Paisley Girl* by Fran Gordon. Copyright © 1999 by Fran Gordon. Reprinted by permission of St. Martin's Press, LLC.

From *My Sister's Bones* by Cathi Hanauer, copyright © 1996 by Cathi Hanauer. Used by permission of Dell Publishing, a division of Random House Inc.

From *Mysterious Skin* by Scott Heim. Copyright © 1995 by Scott Heim. Reprinted by permission of HarperCollins Publishers, Inc.

From *Everything You Know* by Zoë Heller. Copyright © 1999 by Zoë Heller. Reprinted by permission of Alfred A. Knopf, a division of Random House Inc.

Excerpt from *Typical American*. Copyright © 1991 by Gish Jen. Reprinted by permission of Houghton Mifflin Company. All rights reserved.

Excerpt from *Suspicious River*. Copyright © 1996 by Laura Kasischke. Reprinted by permission of Houghton Mifflin Company. All rights reserved.

From *Kink* by Kathe Koja. Copyright © 1996 by Kathe Koja. Published by permission of Kathe Koja c/o Ralph M. Vicinanza, Ltd.

From *Darkness, Take My Hand* by Dennis LeHane. Copyright © 1996 by Dennis LeHane. Reprinted by permission of HarperCollins Publishers, Inc.

From *Motherless Brooklyn* by Jonathan Lethem, copyright © 1999 by Jonathan Lethem. Used by permission of Doubleday, a division of Random House Inc.

Reprinted from *Paradoxia: A Predator's Diary* by Lydia Lunch with the permission of the publishers, Creation Books. Copyright © Lydia Lunch 1997, 1999.

From *The Great Divorce* by Valerie Martin, copyright © 1994 by Valerie Martin. Used by permission of Doubleday, a division of Random House Inc.

From *Like Being Killed* by Ellen Miller, copyright © 1998 by Ellen Miller. Used by permission of Dutton, a division of Penguin Putnam Inc.

From *For Love* by Sue Miller. Copyright © 1993 by Sue Miller. Reprinted by permission of HarperCollins Publishers, Inc.

From *Evening* by Susan Minot. Copyright © 1998 by Susan Minot. Reprinted by permission of Alfred A. Knopf, a division of Random House Inc.

From *Purple America* by Rick Moody. Copyright © 1997 by Rick Moody. By permission of Little, Brown and Company (Inc.).

From *Back Roads* by Tawni O'Dell, copyright © 2000 by Tawni O'Dell. Used by permission of Viking Penguin, a division of Penguin Putnam Inc.

From *Down by the River Where the Dead Men Go* by George P. Pelecanos. Copyright © 1995 by George P. Pelecanos. Reprinted by permission of St. Martin's Press, LLC.

Excerpt from *Rameau's Niece*. Copyright © 1993 by Cathleen Schine. Reprinted by permission of Houghton Mifflin Company. All rights reserved.

From *Rat Bohemia* by Sarah Schulman. Copyright © 1995 by Sarah Schulman. Reprinted by permission of the author.

Reprinted with the permission of Simon & Schuster from *Jumping the Green* by Leslie Schwartz. Copyright © 1999 by Leslie Schwartz.

Reprinted with the permission of Scribner, a division of Simon & Schuster from *The Illusionist* by Dinitia Smith. Copyright © 1997 by Dinitia Smith.

From *Missing Women and Others: Stories* by June Spence, copyright © 1998 by June Spence. Used by permission of Riverhead Books, a division of Penguin Putnam Inc.

From *Jesus Saves* by Darcey Steinke. Copyright © 1997 by Darcey Steinke. Used by permission of Grove/Atlantic, Inc.

From *The Fires* by Rene Steinke. Copyright © 1999 by Rene Steinke. Reprinted by permission of HarperCollins Publishers, Inc.

Excerpt from *Outerbridge Reach*. Copyright © 1992 by Robert Stone. Reprinted by permission of Houghton Mifflin Company. All rights reserved.

From *Brief Interviews with Hideous Men* by David Foster Wallace. Copyright © 1999 by David Foster Wallace. By permission of Little, Brown and Company (Inc.).